Sea

so

Blue

Other works by

Nichole Giles

Descendant
Birthright
Legacy

Water so Deep
Ocean so Wide

Sea so Blue

NICHOLE GILES

First American Paperback Edition

Published by Jelly Bean Press
PO Box 548
Osawatomie, Kansas 66064

ISBN 978-1-63034-049-0

Nichole Giles's author website is http://nicholegiles.net

For my mom, who taught me that everyone deserves a great love story.

Chapter One

VIVID LIGHT CUT THROUGH THE surface of the water, shimmering along Caspian's blue-white skin as his corded muscles drew him ever-closer to shore. Though it had been years since he'd seen the sun, he remembered it from childhood days spent at the beach with the woman from his past—his mother. Long ago, when his father had snatched him from the sandy beach and dragged him beneath the sea, Caspian vowed to escape Atlantis and return to land. He'd lost track of the tide cycles that had passed since he last saw his mother, but the number was many. He'd been smaller then, and far too young for the joining his father now threatened to force upon him with the arrival of the new moon.

Caspian didn't remember her well, but the scattered pieces he could recall left him certain that his mother would not compel him to join with a mermaid he despised.

Still, it wasn't the joining that sent him in search of his past, but the memories that slipped further from his grasp with each passing tide. His human side longed to remember the sensation of walking on feet, warm sand squelching between his toes. To feel the sun heating his skin, and to know the absence of water that would allow his long, dark hair to fall around his shoulders rather than floating above his ears.

And then there was her. Emerald green eyes, hair the color of fire, and soft, smooth arms, ideal for soothing a gloomy child. Memories of her face had faded over time, and he worried about how he would find her, recognize her in a population so vast. He yearned for peace, with his past, his future, and with his place in the world, a muddled position under his current circumstances.

He slowed as he approached the shore, startled and delighted when his ears detected peals of laughter, and a melody, music different from the song of the Mer, though hypnotic in its own way. The beach where he'd last walked had changed dramatically in the time he'd been gone—though, as Caspian glided through the water, he noted the size of his hands, and decided that he had changed as well.

Shops and restaurants had popped up, a boardwalk built. As far as he could see, dwellings consumed the landscape, leaving little space unspoiled with progression.

People crowded into groups under umbrellas and on towels, and some dove into the swells on surfboards or other floatation devices. Nerves sang along his shoulders. He was not a boy anymore, and human customs were little more than a distant memory. He did recall that humans believed the Mer to be legends of mystical and magical proportion, fantasy, but not reality. Perhaps he would be wise to emerge in a place less populated, one that would not create such a spectacle as a merman arising from the sea.

Caspian adjusted his course, aiming for the rocky shoals below the cliffs that towered in the distance. The pearl and seashell necklace, a gift from his cousin, tapped against his chest as he plunged deeper, picking up speed again. If Maui had been successful in the creation of this adornment, it would be the key to Caspian's ability to breathe ashore until he was ready to return home.

His kingdom and his betrothed would be forced to wait while he became reacquainted with the ways of humans. Caspian believed that this knowledge would be of great use when he inherited his father's throne and was charged with the task of ruling Atlantis.

As he approached the shoals, the water shallowed, the coast below the cliffs littered with boulders and land-masses, which created a natural inlet. Set back from the populated section of beach, this uninhabited inlet led into a shallow cave, carved into the side of the cliff, and invisible from land. Instead of beach, sharp, pitted rocks and tide pools made up the semi-level ground. The only sand he could see was the soft, white powder lining the inside of the cave.

He pulled himself onto the rocky shore, marveling at the heat that dried his hands before he lifted the rest of his body from the sea. Overhanging land far above provided ample shade, sheltering the spot from sight, and further limiting the possibility of humans visiting the secluded space. In the distant sky, far above him, a shining creature flew, cutting the blue expanse with a thick, white trail. Something about the creature seemed familiar to Caspian, but words and details wisped from his brain as the delicate skeins of newly formed coral.

The golden sun hung high overhead, stinging the white-blue skin on his shoulders, nose, and feet. He scooted into the shade of the shallow cavity, grateful to find the sand cooler here, in the same way that the sea chilled with each foot of depth that generated distance between his body and the rays from above.

As his fin dried, his legs separated, and the webbing between his toes thinned, curling into the creases. Caspian pressed his feet to the sand and, using the rough stone walls for balance, made a wobbly attempt to stand.

Muscles he had forgotten existed tightened, from the bottoms of his feet, through his calves and into his knees, thighs, and hips, and he marveled at the sensation of feeling his weight balanced on two feet that seemed so much smaller than a fin.

At times, he'd used his feet to stand in Atlantis, but never for long, and never with any dependency or need. Mostly, it had been an old habit from his youth that sometimes reared up and required the use of his standing muscles. But such occasions had been rare, and standing underwater had never required that his feet alone hold his entire mass.

As if to prove such a deed impossible, he tipped to one side, smacking his knee and an elbow against the rough rocks as he slammed on his backside into the sand. Pain jolted up his spine and left his head spinning. He tried again, taking care with the placement of his feet, this time spreading them far enough apart to create more stability.

He inhaled a breath of air, remembering as he did, that such a thing required the use of his nose and mouth, rather than the deep gills cut into the sides of his throat. Again, the sensation struck him as both strange and familiar. Two more breaths gave him confidence that the pendant had worked, so he attempted to take first one step, and then two. Each time his feet hit the ground, his bones rattled from the force.

On the third step, he snapped his teeth on his tongue and, screaming in pain, leapt around the cave, spitting out blood until he once again lost balance, and ended on his back in the sand, staring up at the jagged ceiling.

Being human wasn't coming as naturally as he'd expected. For a moment, he questioned the plan he had conjured after an informative visit from his cousin, Maui. Then he remembered his upcoming joining to Marietta, the cunning, demanding, and strangely shaped mermaid, chosen by his father to become Caspian's bride, and determined to continue his quest.

During one of their many conversations, Maui had spoken about coverings that humans draped over their bodies, much as the Mer of Atlantis draped adornments around their necks and wrists and in their hair. At the time, Caspian had managed to grasp onto a vague memory of such coverings, and even somehow remembered the word clothes.

He glanced down at the body that appeared human, with the exception of a few scales lingering on the backs of his knees, his ankles, and upper thighs, and tried to conjure a memory of the coverings he'd worn as a youngling. The only one that came to mind was a bright cloth that concealed him from knee to waist as he darted into the ocean to frolic in the waves.

It was a lucky thing, then, that Maui had supplied him with clothes and instructed him on how to use them. Caspian opened the netted cargo trap in which he'd carried his supplies—strapped to his waist as he swam—and pulled out the odd garments. The first one was soft and damp, and had three holes at the top and a larger one on the bottom. The second reminded him of the covering he'd worn in the waves, which helped as he pulled them on, one leg at a time.

The wet fabric stuck to his skin, reminding him of his ocean home, and comforting him in a way he didn't realize coverings could. Perhaps he would enjoy this part of being human. The remaining covering proved slightly trickier to master, but once he got his head into the largest hole at the top, he figured the other two were meant for his arms, and that seemed to work, as it left his entire torso covered where the bottom garment left off.

With the coverings in place, Caspian withdrew from his sack two gold pieces he'd salvaged from a shipwreck, and the stone tablet in which he'd etched the human characters Maui had given him to help find his mother. He did remember some letters and numbers, but could not make heads or tails of the way they'd been etched, so he was forced to trust that another human could—and that his cousin had not led him astray.

After more practice walking, he peeked around the edges of the cave, searching for a way up the steep, rocky incline to the civilization above, and when he found a precipitous, pitted path, made his way up. The bright sun pressed hot against his skin, changing any remaining blue to white, and bringing forth beads of salt water that dripped down his back and over his forehead. Thick air weighed heavier in his lungs than water passing through his gills. But his chest thrummed a quick and steady rhythm in a way it hadn't since the younger version of himself had gone on a secret swim with a mermaid who was not his betrothed, and they'd been cornered by a pod of sharks.

According to Maui, the humans he sought were not so vicious as sharks, but could be far more dangerous than the strongest, scariest predators in the sea when provoked, and too often, fear became action, without input from reason or thought.

He reached the top of the cliff, met with the pleasant shade of tall, green trees, which allowed him to catch his breath and slow his heart before he began again and discovered dwellings, and a road.

One task accomplished, he thought. *I have covered my body and remembered how to walk. And now to find my mother.*

Chapter Two

"I'M TAKING MY BREAK!" ELISE Shannon hung her apron on a hook and opened the steel-fronted commercial fridge, unburying the flowers she'd hidden behind the hamburger toppings.

Marcus dinged the bell and yelled, "Order up," at Shelley, who snatched the plate and nearly tossed the contents on the ground—luckily saving it at the last minute so she could deliver it to table twelve. He pressed his spatula against the burgers sizzling on the cooktop and shook his head at Elise. "Hurry back, would ya? I don't trust the new girl to keep up with the early dinner rush."

Elise slung her purse over her shoulder, digging out her keys one-handed. "She's getting there, Marcus. It's only been two weeks. Give her some slack."

"I do. I just need her to know all of this yesterday." He wiped his forehead with a huge white handkerchief and then shoved it back in the pocket where he kept it. "You sure you don't know anyone else looking for a job? We've got to fill that other position if you want to have a day off anytime in the next year."

"All my friends have gone away for college." Dark clouds of despair hovered too close, so she stuck her face in the flowers and inhaled. *I'm okay. I'm going to keep being okay.* "There's no one left."

Marcus inhaled a sharp breath. "You've got me, little bird. I promised your daddy I'd look after you. You're not alone."

Elise forced a smile that didn't reach her eyes as she pushed through the backdoor into the alley. Marcus meant well, but it didn't help when he continually reminded her how much she'd lost in the last few months.

She brushed the dust off the windshield of her father's partially-restored '66 Mustang convertible, grateful that it ran, even if the body still needed work. The engine rumbled to life, and Elise tore out of the parking lot, frustrated that she felt rushed, especially today, of all days.

Sunlight gleamed off the rusty metal hood, sending spots of light to bounce around the car as she pulled onto the narrow lane that led to the antique church. She drove as far as the road would take her, and then hiked to the top corner of the grassy knoll, where the familiar headstone lay, embedded in the overgrown grass. A viney weed crept over the granite, so Elise pulled it as she knelt, and replaced the weed with the fresh flowers she'd brought.

She ran her fingers over her mother's name, trying to remember the face that went with it. A faded picture on her dresser was all she had left of the woman who had died on this exact day, the year Elise was four, and now she'd lost her father, too. Tears gathered in her eyes as she brushed dust off the newly carved name, and she fought the instinct to curl in a ball and bury herself next to her parents. Only six months had passed since her father died, and yet so much had changed, it felt like a lifetime already. "I miss you, Daddy." She stroked the headstone as if doing so would encourage a visit from his spirit, allowing them to talk, one last time. "I graduated last month. Wasn't sure I'd make it after you left me, but I knew how important education was to you, so I pushed through. Not honors or anything, but I got all my credits, which felt like a miracle toward the end."

A bird trilled at the top of the trees, and another answered, reminding Elise that she had no one left to respond to her calls. She swallowed emotion building in her throat. "Still working for Marcus. He's given me insane hours since Jenny quit, but I need the money, so I can't complain." The small amount of life insurance she'd received had gone toward paying off the cottage where she'd grown up. Since then, she'd managed to pay the power and water bills, but no longer had a phone, cable, or internet. Gas and food had become priority, and TV a luxury meant for those who had time to sit.

Now that she'd finished high school and was able to work more hours, she had a lofty goal of saving up for a pay-as-you go cell phone for emergencies. She figured having it would make her feel better about being alone in the house on stormy nights.

"Rachel moved to the east coast last week, so she can study acting while she gets her business degree." She giggled at how strange a concept the two ideas seemed together. "Guess she wants to keep her options open. And Laura took that internship in Spain. Remember how much of a long-shot we thought that was? Guess the program wasn't as tough to get into as we thought."

Both friends had invited Elise to come with them. Rachel had even reminded her how little she had left in Oceanside, but Elise couldn't leave. Her objections weren't only about money—though money was a large part. She'd grown up believing that she'd travel to fancy and exotic places after high school, but profound loss had left her longing to hold tightly to everything familiar, and her father's house, his car, even his antique pocket watch—she simply couldn't let them go.

Not yet. Maybe not ever. These things were all she had left of her family, and family was something she ached to have again.

"Marcus thinks I could get financial aid and go to school here, if I want," she continued. "But I'm thinking of taking a couple of semesters off to build my savings. Would be nice to have an emergency cushion." She couldn't bring herself to tell her parents that she was considering forgoing college indefinitely, even if they couldn't truly hear. Somehow saying the words made it more real, and everything about her life right now felt more like a dream than reality. "Don't worry, Daddy. I won't sell your car. Had a collector offer me a ridiculously low amount last week, and decided that even if he offered me millions, I couldn't do it. You love that car, and it's all I have left of you. I just hope it keeps running for a few more years."

Her watch alarm beeped, signaling that it was time to head back to work, before Marcus freaked out on poor Shelley. Elise wiped moisture from her cheeks, sniffling as she stood. "I don't know what I'm doing, or where my life is going, but I promise that no matter what, I'll find a way to make you both proud."

As she always did, Elise hummed her father's favorite Guns and Roses song as she trudged down the hill to the car, eyes focused on the uneven ground to avoid tripping on a headstone hidden beneath the weeds.

The remote, sparsely populated cemetery had been her father's choice when they buried her mother, because he thought it a peaceful and serene place of rest, away from busy streets and industrial noise. Elise agreed, grateful that when she visited, it seemed as if her parents were the only people buried here, and when she talked to them, no one in the world besides them could hear. Trees dotted the landscape and kept the grass green and shaded, and when the grounds keeper stayed away too long, allowing weeds to grow thick and lush, Elise imagined her parents vacationing in a verdant jungle. It helped to know that anything could thrive here.

She reached the road, startled to find a tall, dark-haired man staring at her car as if completely befuddled by it. The symmetrical bones in his face might have been carved from stone, and the eyes that focused so intently on her car, blinked an astonishing shade of deep green. His long, thick hair appeared to be wet, sticking to his T-shirt halfway down his back. That T-shirt was on inside-out and backwards, only a step behind the dripping basketball shorts sticking to the red, irritated skin on his legs. He wore no shoes, and stood on the edges of his feet, teetering from side-to-side like a toddler learning to walk.

"Hi." She stood near the hood of her car, keeping it as a barrier between them. "You seem lost. Can I help you find something? Or someone, maybe?"

Those green eyes snapped to Elise, locking onto her face. "I am looking for my mother."

That explains a lot. Sympathy flooded her system, sending her into the protective, mother-hen mode she'd adopted when she'd first learned that her father was sick. "Do you remember where she's buried?"

The man blinked, his mouth rolling the word buried around as if it was a foreign language.

Elise twisted her hands together, keys dangling from one finger. "What's her name?"

"My mother?" He stepped away, seeming nervous in ways she could only imagine, and severely disoriented.

His grief must be fresh, then. "How long has she been gone?"

"She is not gone. I am here to find her."

Elise's watch beeped again. She had to go, but seeing how distressed this man appeared, she hesitated to leave him alone. Clearly, he was suffering tremendous loss. A loss with which she could sympathize. She reached out a hand, palm up, in a gesture of friendship. "My name's Elise. I'd love to stay and help you, but I really have to get back to work. Can I drop you somewhere?"

He stared at her outstretched hand, and then, as if realizing something, dropped a tarnished coin into it. "At my mother's house. Please."

The formal way with which he'd presented the quarter only further confused Elise. Maybe he needed to be taken to a hospital. "Where does your mother live?"

"On land," he said, confidence filling his voice. "In a stone dwelling."

Okay, he's definitely snapped. Unwilling to leave the confused stranger standing in the middle of a cemetery with no idea who he was or where he was going, Elise reached around and opened the passenger door, waving him inside. "Will you come with me? I'll *try* to help you find your mother."

His wobbly steps landed heavily on the ground, digging rocks into his bare feet, but the confused man didn't seem to notice as he sat heavily on the seat in her car. "Thank you."

"You're welcome." She closed his door, dropping the coin into her pocket as she withdrew her keys and settled on the driver's seat. "Have you eaten? I work at a beach-side diner not far from here, and I need to go there before we look for your mother. I'm happy to buy you a burger."

"A burger?" He squinted against the glare of the hood through the windshield, covering his eyes as if the brightness was too much for him. "I do not know that word."

Elise started the engine, baffled that such a person existed. Who didn't know about hamburgers? "It's food. You'll like it, trust me."

"Food. I would be happy for nourishment." As they rolled down the lane and pulled onto the road, the man pressed his face against the window glass, seeming fascinated by everything they passed.

I just let a stranger into my car, and he's obviously not stable. Elise could hear her father lecturing her from the beyond about personal safety, but something in the man's eyes drew her in and refused to set her free. "What's your name?" she asked, deciding that at least she could stop thinking of him as *the man* or *mysterious cemetery stranger.*

He straightened, rising to an impressive height. "I am Caspian."

"Caspian," she repeated, liking the way it sounded to her ears, the way it rolled off her tongue. "That's a great name. Unique."

"Thank you. Elise is also a good name. Strong, like the current, and delicate as a seahorse's coronet."

Well, aren't you the charmer? "Seahorses are my favorite. So tiny and sweet." She faced the road, but her eyes flicked sideways for a stolen glance at the handsome, mysterious stranger—Caspian. His wet clothes clung to his skin, outlining corded muscles covering every inch of his body. Despite his current bedraggled appearance, she couldn't imagine that he was homeless, unless he'd lost his home recently enough that he hadn't yet grown a beard. Maybe letting him in her car had been the wrong thing to do, but

Caspian continued to fascinate Elise for reasons she couldn't fathom, other than that he had recently suffered a loss similar to the one she'd suffered six months ago, and for that, she had mountains of sympathy.

They pulled into the alley behind The Sea Turtle Café and bar, the restaurant where she'd been working since she was a freshman in high school—back when life was easy and her most important goal was to earn enough money for a pair of popular designer jeans and some great shoes. She parked the car and opened Caspian's door—since he didn't seem inclined to do so himself—hoping Marcus wouldn't be mad at her for bringing a stranger through his kitchen—and then led him inside.

Immediately, Caspian stopped and inhaled. "What is that . . . interesting aroma? Is a creature dying?"

Despite what must be a gloomy situation, Elise burst out laughing. "It's Marcus's infamous turtle burgers. Bestseller on popular beach days. All days, really."

"How many turtles has this Marcus killed to cause such a stench?" Despite his use of the word stench, he continued forward, nose in the air as if allowing it to lead him.

Elise caught Caspian's arm to keep him from crashing into the production station where Marcus assembled each dish. "None. It's called a turtle burger because that's the name of the restaurant."

His brow bunched with confusion, but he didn't comment further, instead focusing on the pink shrimp Marcus had marinating in his specialty sauce. "I've never seen a pink species of shrimp before. This is remarkable." He picked a shrimp out with his fingers and dropped it into his mouth, frowning at the result. "Mushy. Not right. These pink ones taste all wrong. They have no skin."

"Elise, keep your friend's fingers out of my food! Now I have to throw that whole batch away." Marcus stormed to the metal table and snatched up the tub of shrimp, glaring at Caspian.

Caspian blinked, eyes wide and astonished. "I am sorry to displease the Burger King, sir. Please do not order me to your dungeons. I do not believe I could withstand the odor in such a place."

Marcus dumped the shrimp into the trash and rounded on Elise. "Is this guy serious? Who is he, and what is he doing in my kitchen?"

With Caspian settled at a table where she could keep an eye on him, Elise dragged Marcus away from his stove. "I don't know what to do with him," she explained. "He was at the cemetery, wandering like a homeless puppy, and talking about how he needs to find his mother. I'm almost surprised he remembers his name."

Marcus waved his spatula in the direction of the dining room. "So you brought him here? What do you think this is, a homeless shelter?"

At his table across the room, Caspian poked at his burger with a finger, then lifted the bun and licked it, frowning. "That's just it, Marcus, I don't think he's homeless."

"Smells like he is." Marcus returned to his cooktop and flipped the burgers, adding a slice of specialty cheese and a tomato and covered them with a lid. "Can't believe you brought him into my kitchen. Do you have any idea the kind of germs he could be spreading?"

Elise wasn't as worried about germs so much as this person's serious mental issues. "He seems so lost."

"You said that already." Marcus plated a toasted bun, spread his secret sauce, then scooped a burger onto it and layered lettuce, pineapple, and red onion before finishing the tower with his sweet shrimp concoction. A toothpick in the middle and a side of fries, and he slid the plate across the counter and dinged the bell for Shelley. "Look, Elise, you're a nurturer. You nurtured your father through his sickness, and through all the years after you lost your mom—I'm sure it's mostly instinct. But this guy needs the kind of help only a doctor can give him, and you're not a doctor."

Elise leaned against the assembly station, careful to avoid getting anywhere near the food. "I know, Marcus. And I'm going to take him to the emergency room mental department as soon as my shift is over. I wanted to feed him first, and not keep you waiting if the lunch rush got bad. You were already frustrated with Shelley."

Marcus assembled another burger, nearly identical to the first. "And see how much work I'm getting from you now that you're here? Absolutely none."

Taking the hint, Elise snagged her apron off the hook and swiped her hair out of her eyes. "Made it back before the crowd. Even on the anniversary of my mother's death. You're welcome."

As she sauntered into the dining room, Marcus called to her, "You just remember what I told you, Elise. Doctors require a lot more schooling than your shiny-new high school degree."

Chapter Three

THE TEXTURE OF THIS FOOD *is like a sponge.* Caspian poked at the hamburger bun, digging into his memory for the word that he knew belonged to this food. A vague connection to his childhood came as he recalled sitting on the beach, eating something similar and feeding pieces of it to seagulls as they flocked around him on the sand.

"Bah . . . brrr." He picked up the bun and sniffed it again, then took a bite, and the word flooded into his mind as if he'd opened a gate. "Bread." He took another bite, then another, eventually shoving the entire top-half into his mouth at once. Though the pink shrimp he'd tasted in the kitchen weren't his favorite, he picked them off, one-by-one, and shoved them in his mouth as well, realizing it had been days since he'd eaten. The flat, brown meat beneath the shrimp seemed far less attractive, as the smell reminded him of the palace galley, where they cleaned and deboned the fish and prepared meals.

Still, determined to find more memories, he picked up that meat between his fingers and nibbled at the edge, finding the flavor not as unappealing as he had expected. This meat—whatever it was—had much flavor and caused his stomach to rumble with pleasure as he consumed it in three bites.

The female who had promised to take him to his mother arrived, wearing a new adornment around her middle, and offered him a vessel filled with water. Since the bread stuck to his teeth like the suckers of an octopus, he snatched the vessel and gulped, gulped, gulped until the water had been drained. The female, Elise, settled on the chair across from him.

"Thank you for the nourishment," he told her. "I am ready to be taken to my mother, now."

"About that." Elise inhaled a deep breath and let it out slowly. "The thing is, I don't know where your mother is buried. Maybe if you remember her name, we can call the cemetery and get a location for the grave."

"Her name is Momma." Confidence oozed through his every word, though the female's eyebrows pinched together in dismay. Still, he knew. That was what he'd called her, and what others had called her as well, despite his being an only child. Momma.

"I know." Her slim fingers tap-tap-tapped on the table, reminding him of a parrotfish crunching on fresh coral. She leaned closer, her bright blue eyes piercing the scales his body continued to shed. "Caspian, do you know how long your mother has been gone?"

He replayed the memory of his final moments with her in a continued loop in his head, and had since the day Maui arrived in Atlantis. How she'd seemed so happy at first, until his father had snatched him away from her and rocketed back to the sea. The sound of her screams continued to haunt him, even now. "Many, many tides. I was small."

She bit her plump bottom lip, chewing on it hard enough that Caspian worried she'd gnaw it right off, as a dying sea-lion might. "Do you know where you live? I just . . . I'm not sure what to do with you right now."

The drumming stopped, and her fingers found their way to the top of his hand, where her tender, silky strokes sent flames through his scales and all the way to his toes, erasing all other thoughts from his mind. His attention snapped to her face, where long, dark lashes swept over deep-set, sea-blue eyes. Blink, blink. Blink. His tongue rolled into his throat, his mouth parched and longing for another vessel of water to wash the dryness away.

"Elise, order up!" The shout came from the man in the kitchen, the one who had bellowed at him for tasting the chewy shrimps. Elise stood, her gaze lingering on the place where their skin had touched.

"Getting cold," the man hollered. "Sometime today, please."

"I have to get back to work." Elise stumbled, her eyes flicking back to Caspian's one last time. "Don't go anywhere, okay? I'm off in two hours. We'll figure something out, then."

He waited for what seemed an infinite amount of time, yet as Elise scuttled between tables and counter, he decided he would be happy to observe her actions for many tides. The way her sun-kissed skin shimmered under the bright lights as she hefted tray after tray, dancing across the floor to deliver each item to the smiling, happy humans she served. The way her copper hair floated around her shoulders, waving gently across her neck and down her back. Her adept ability to avoid dropping a towering of dirty dishes, muscle-toned limbs keeping the teetering porcelain aloft when a toddler flopped to the floor at her feet. The way she smiled at each individual, her eyes sparkling as she silently vowed to make their meal a pleasant one.

Long after the sun had dipped beneath the sea, leaving the sky as dark as the deepest caverns, she removed the adornment from her waist and returned to sit in the spot she'd occupied before. Her cheeks filled with air, letting it out slowly, and her shoulders and chest sank with exhaustion. "How do you feel about coming home with me for the night?"

Warmth filled his chest. She wished to help him, to keep him safe and serve him as she had served all the others who had come into her care on this day. "I find that an acceptable arrangement. But only if you will take me to my mother after that."

Her lips pressed into a tight line. "You're not from around here, are you?"

Confusion bounced in his brain. *How could she know such a thing?* "I come from a faraway land."

The sparkle returned to her eyes as she reached out and, again, placed her hand over his on the table. "That explains a lot. Your accent isn't bad, but you definitely don't talk like the locals."

Worry tightened his chest as he recalled his father's grave warning before Caspian had left Atlantis. *No one must ever know where you've been, or to where you shall return. If ever a human discovers your secret, the results will be as if a school of sharks tore your body to shreds.*

Elise must never know of Atlantis, he thought. *I will not allow her to become as shark bait.* "My home lies across the blue sea, near the place where fire lights the sky."

She squeezed the bridge of her nose, shaking her head. "You know, you really aren't making this easy for me." The lights dimmed, and the other female worked, swiping crumbs from each table into a long tray. Elise stood. "I'm going to help clean up, and then we can leave. I'll just be a few more minutes."

Even knowing she would return to him shortly, instinct urged him to keep her near. "Might I trouble you for more water?"

Another large, slow breath, causing her chest to rise and fall again. "Of course." She turned to walk away, and though he'd been watching her for many long hours, marveled at the way her hips swayed when she moved. He had not yet found his mother, but in the time that he'd been ashore, Caspian had already learned quite a bit about the humans he'd come to study.

Chapter Four

"IT'S NOT THE RITZ CARLTON, but better than
sleeping on the street." Elise turned her key in the lock
and flipped on the light in the entry, dropping her
keys, purse, and shoes just inside. Noticing, again,
Caspian's bare feet, she decided that maybe it was time
to venture into her father's closet—the one space she'd
yet to clear, or even to open, since the day of the
funeral.

"I find this dwelling suitable. It reminds me of my
mother's home." Caspian stood rigid next to the door,
taking in every detail of the cottage.

She dropped onto the couch and kicked her aching
feet onto the coffee table, wishing she could afford the
luxury of a foot massage. Just her feet would suit her
fine. "Mine, too. This actually *was* my mother's home,

and my father's. I grew up here, and now that they're gone, it's mine."

On the wall near the door, Elise had hung a large, framed print of her parents, each holding one of her tiny hands as they walked on a beach. Caspian's gaze landed on the photo, lighting up as if it somehow gave him answers to his own woes. He pressed his fingertips to the glass and dragged them across it, his throat moving as he swallowed. "This. I remember something like this. My mother had a similar one in which I sat on the beach, feeding on handfuls of wet sand."

His memories came in bits and pieces that left her wondering how much trauma he'd endured to break what was clearly a highly intelligent mind. She stood and joined him in his study of her family. "What about your father? Was he in the picture as well? Is he still with you?"

Caspian's eyes darkened, and he turned his back on the picture. "His image was not, though my mother claimed that I bore a strong resemblance. I did not know my father then."

Tread carefully, Elise. You're hitting on a nerve. His clothes had long-since dried, and crunched a bit when he moved, yet he still had not asked to use her shower. Her stomach leapt with anxiety. As they'd left the Turtle, she'd promised Marcus that she'd take Caspian to the hospital. And yet, everything about him seemed innocent and sweet, his body strong, yet his mind fragmented. Unable to shake her fascination with this anomaly of a man, she'd driven straight past the hospital and done the one thing she'd sworn to her father she would never do. She drove a stranger to her home and let him inside.

Fortunately for her, she'd learned to rely heavily on her instincts, and right now she sensed absolutely zero danger. A relief, to be certain. She only hoped this didn't become the one time she was wrong.

Caspian's rigid stance shifted, and sand particles rained onto the tile entry. "I should let you get cleaned up." Elise turned on more lights and waved for Caspian to follow her to the bathroom, where she dug out the fluffiest towel she could find and handed it to him. Caspian accepted the towel, staring at it as if he had no clue what it was for, so she clarified as she dug out soap, shampoo, and a spare toothbrush she'd saved from her last dental visit. "I assume you'd like to take a shower? It's important to wash the salt off your skin, or you could end up with a rash."

Another spark of knowledge flashed in his expression. "A shower. Yes, thank you."

When he remained in the hall, back rigid and shoulders squared, it occurred to Elise why he might be hesitant. She set the supplies on the towel. "If you'll give me a moment, I'll find you something clean to wear." She scooted around Caspian's wide presence in the narrow hallway, and into the master bedroom, and the closet she hadn't opened in months. Simply touching the doorknob sent torrents of grief through her, but, the presence of Caspian and his broken mind gave her strength to push past her sadness, and she swung the door open, flicking on the light.

Dust had gathered on the shoulders of his shirts and coated his dark shoes with a film of white, and an empty hanger swung in place of his favorite navy-blue suit, but nothing else had changed. She inhaled a deep breath, absorbing the lingering scent of cologne and masculine shampoo, surprised to find comfort in such a small memory. She chose a pair of her father's pajama pants and a T-shirt and shut the door again, tenderly hiding away the pain of her in-home memorial.

By the time she returned to the bathroom, Caspian had already closed himself in. She raised her fist to knock. "Caspian, I've brought you some pajamas. I'll just leave them outside the door." She couldn't hear the water running yet, so when he didn't reply, she kept talking. "I'd be happy to run your clothes through the wash, if you want. You can get them to me when you're finished showering."

She laid the pajamas on the floor, and the bathroom door swung open, revealing a strapping body—carved from curve upon curve of taught muscle, covered in skin so white that the reflection of the bathroom lights flashed from every glistening bend—all six feet of bare skin. He wore only a necklace of pearls and seashells that accented his firm trap muscles. Elise's mouth fell open as she dragged her eyes up to his face, compelling herself to keep them there, though the temptation to inspect the rest of him burned strong. "Hi." Her voice squeaked, though she couldn't decide if it was from shock or nerves or all-out lust.

He'd wadded his clothes into a tight ball and held them in his hand, which he extended to her. "I thank you for assisting me with my coverings. They had begun to feel stiff and unnatural."

Elise stumbled backward, breath quickening as she accepted the crunchy bundle. "I . . . you didn't have to . . . I could've waited until you were finished and," unable to stop herself, her eyes flicked down his body, then back up again, "dressed."

"Dressed? But did you not request to clean my clothes?"

"Yes. I suppose I did." While Elise fumbled for footing, for words, for breath, Caspian tilted his head, glorified in his humble masculinity, and unfazed about standing naked in the presence of a virtual stranger. When she backed into the wall, he leapt forward and lifted her by the elbows as if to save her from crashing to the ground, and replaced her on her feet. "Are you all right?"

With his bare chest mere inches from her face, and his other parts far too close for her to ignore, she nodded a mute yes and tucked his clothes beneath her arm.

Noticing the pajamas she'd set on the ground, he picked them up, his face illuminating with pleasure as he ran his fingers over the soft cotton and flannel. "When you see me next, Elise of the land, I shall be cleaned and dressed, awaiting our next adventure together."

Elise blinked, at a complete loss for words as Caspian closed himself in the bathroom with a soft click. If nothing else, the evening would be interesting.

He emerged an hour later and joined her on the couch in the living room, fresh and clean, and filling out her father's pajamas in ways her father never could have, damp hair once again waving down his back. "Did you have a nice shower?"

"The falling water provided my skin with glorious sensations, though I didn't much like the suds caused by the substance you provided for my hair."

Elise had to press her lips together to keep from laughing as she adjusted her position to sit sideways. "Do you not use shampoo where you're from?"

He adjusted as well, this time struggling with the word shampoo. Elise wondered if she'd ever understand how such simple things caused him so much confusion. "I remember something comparable from my childhood. But I have not known such a luxury since I saw my mother last."

"I wish you remembered her better." A wet tress of hair stuck to Caspian's neck, reminding Elise of just how much she'd seen of him. When he didn't move it immediately, she longed to do it for him, to peel the dark strand off his neck and brush it behind his shoulder with the rest of his thick, undamaged mane.

The skin around his eyes pulled tight as he frowned, shifting in his seat again. "I plan to know more of her once I locate her dwelling."

The hair, still stuck to his neck, had kept Elise so rapt that processing his words required seconds longer than normal. When they registered, she inched closer, as if better proximity would clarify her confusion. "Wait. I thought we were looking for a grave. Caspian, is your mother still . . . alive?"

One corner of his lips twitched, as if smiling was as foreign to him as he was to Oceanside. "Oh yes. If she was not, my father would never have allowed me to visit."

Uh, you're a grown man. "Allowed you to visit." She shook her head, relaxing against the couch, head to lolling back so she could stare at the ceiling. "I'm so confused right now."

36

"I am also confused." Caspian stood and crossed to the fireplace mantle, inspecting the selection of seashells that she and her father had collected over the years. He picked up a smooth brown and white one, shaped like a cone.

"That's an alphabet cone," Elise told him, standing to join him. "My father and I found it on a beach in Florida while vacationing a few years back." She picked up the next one, a bulbous one with a single spiny wing. "This one is called lace murex, because it looks delicate and fragile, like lace, but is really all spines and points. We got this one on the gulf coast in Texas."

Caspian ran his fingers along a smooth, swirling shell coated with a lovely mix of chocolate and cream colors. "What do you call this one?"

"Shark's eye moon shell." Elise also ran her fingers over the smooth surface, jolting when her fingers brushed his and sent a rod of fire into her veins.

Caspian lifted the shell to cover his eye. "Do I appear as a shark now? Watching you and planning my attack?"

A shiver crept up her spine. They'd been together for more than half the day, and this was the first attempt Caspian had made at a joke. She doubted that he'd intended for his words to come across as a cheesy pickup line, but part of her wished it was exactly that. "Not even a little bit."

His arm dropped to his side, but his gaze stayed on Elise. "Everything about this place feels strange to me. Even objects that are familiar to my eyes, objects I see and pass and touch all the time, contain a new meaning while I am here in your dwelling. With you."

The breath stalled in her chest while her brain attempted to keep pace with Caspian's ups and downs and side-to-sides. The way his brain bounced from topic-to-topic had proven dizzying. And that same lock of hair remained stuck to his neck. Unable to focus on anything else, she extended a gentle hand and stripped it away from his skin, her fingers grazing his neck, scuffing the edge of his necklace, and then trailing over his shoulder as heat sparked across her shoulders and into her toes. Caspian gasped, his muscles tightening and back going rigid.

He feels it too. She dropped her hand as heat crept into her cheeks. "Sorry, that's been making me sort of crazy."

His fingers encircled her wrist and brought her hand back to his shoulder, and, with her help, splayed it across his firmly defined chest. "I relish the sensation caused when our bodies connect in this way."

Coming from any other man, that comment would have sent up a bouquet of red flags, but not from Caspian. Somehow, her every instinct contended that his innocence came from truth, reality.

No one could be this good of an actor, even in the movies. Unfortunately, movies like this tended to end tragically. She hoped her time with Caspian would not follow that pattern.

Chapter Five

THE MOMENT HER FINGERS BRUSHED his skin, her eyes fluttered and closed, causing waves of desire to crash around him. In all his life, he had never met a female—mermaid or human—with eyes as wide and blue as the sea, and a voice more hypnotic than mermaid song. He longed for her to touch more of him, to have those fingertips penetrate the scales that continued to slough off his body, and find the soft skin beneath.

And then he longed for . . . something more, though he wasn't sure exactly what.

Elise was human, and he a prince of Atlantis, betrothed for a joining upon his return. Since his first days in the below, his father had drilled into him all the ways in which a prince should behave, the most important rule being that he should not unite with a maid until they had been joined by royal decree of the Sea King. He had been tempted to disobey this most solemn of oaths on more than one occasion, but never had temptation given him reason to risk this rule.

Her breath shuddered and she blinked, eyes cloudy and confused. "I don't know what's happening to me."

The way she rolled her head, dazed in a way she hadn't been moments ago, sent alarm shooting through his system. Maui had warned Caspian that he might draw in females with extra strong pheromones during his first days on land, and from the way this female reacted, it became apparent that Maui's theory had been correct. Though Caspian wanted nothing more than to explore his fascination with Elise, he could not, in good conscience, push forward while the additional pheromones drew her in—especially since he would only know her for a short time. He drew away, cutting off the ability for either of them to touch the other again. "I am sorry. I should not do such things when you have brought me into your home and served me as a friend."

"Don't be sorry." Elise's cheeks flushed pink, and her shoulders slumped as she stepped away. "I should get to bed. Let me show you to my father's . . . I mean, your room. My father doesn't live there anymore, and no one sleeps in that bed. Just you. Tonight, anyway."

The chemistry that had sprung between them shattered as Elise directed him to a chamber at the end

41

of the hall, and a large, square sleeping platform big enough that three, or even four, Mer could have rested upon it.

"I changed the bedding while you showered, so it's all fresh." With her back to him, she retrieved a bundle from a chair, but didn't turn to face him. "Wasn't sure how many blankets you'd want, so I only put two on the bed, but here are two more if you need them. The days have been warm, but sometimes the evenings can get chilly."

Though he hadn't joined with a maid, Caspian had courted his share of females while his father negotiated a mate. The way Elise stood, head down, eyes focused on the wooden floor, shoulders curved toward her chest, expressed a universal language. His rejection of her stung.

His feet had carried him to her, and his hands reached, insides begging him to remove her hurt.

Her hair fell forward, revealing a slender, smooth neck, free of gills or other markings, save a smattering of tiny brown dots in a variety of sandy browns. His eyes riveted on those dots, fingers itching to draw lines between them and discover their true shape.

His father's voice rang in his memory. *No one.*

The strength he'd witnessed in Elise on this day was great. He imagined what might happen were she to be plunged into a school of sharks—it would not be something she could survive. The idea of razor-sharp teeth tearing into her tender flesh caused revulsion to pulse in his muscles, so he stepped back without touching her, and said nothing. She turned, eyes bright. Too bright. Deceptively joyful. Air caught in Caspian's throat as if a fish bone had lodged there, and the part of him that remained Mer sought to breathe through gills that were currently sealed. Though he could not fathom why, knowing he had hurt Elise stabbed like the barb of a ray, rattling through is chest as he gasped.

The idea of hurting Marietta had never bothered him so.

Alarmed, Elise dropped her bundle and pounded on his chest. "Are you okay? Do you need some water?"

Caspian could not speak to reply, but moments later, Elise pressed a vessel of water to his lips and he drank until the choking subsided. His chest continued to burn, but he forced himself to speak. "Thank you for your assistance this day. It will not be forgotten."

The chill returned to her eyes, but she blinked it away so fast, Caspian wondered if he'd imagined it. "You're welcome. Please make yourself at home. You know where the bathroom is, and the kitchen, so . . . Whatever you need is yours. No need to ask."

Never before had another creature—of any variety—offered him everything she had, asking no promises in return. This was not something he understood in the least, but gratitude rose in his entire being. "Good sleep, Elise."

She backed into the hall, hand on the doorknob. "Goodnight, Caspian."

Once the door clicked shut, Caspian returned to the bundle and picked it up by grabbing hold of two opposite folds. The small bundle unfurled into a soft, sleeping cloth. Recollections of his childhood pushed at his memory, hands, dragging such a cloth over him in the dark, brushing his short hair across his forehead, and lips pressing against his cheek. "Blanket," he said, demanding the memory to solidify and take shape, but even as he sprawled over the platform and sank into the cloud-like surface, even as he dragged the cloth over himself, the memory gate refused to open any further.

He closed his eyes, the wave of nostalgia strong enough to cause a burn in his throat. He could not have Elise. She would never be an option. But he could see his mother again, and that would have to be good enough.

Ribbons of bright light splashed across his face, burning through his eyelids and forcing him awake. Caspian sat up, having lost the blanket covering as he slept, and finding it pooled in a heap on the floor. He stretched his tender feet toward the ground and, using the bed for leverage, pushed himself up. This time, walking came more naturally, and though the muscles in his thighs ached from exertion from the day before, satisfaction pushed him out the door and into the kitchen.

Elise had not yet emerged from her chamber, so Caspian hunted her supply of food, confused by the choices available until he happened upon a package of cold, pink crab-legs. He removed the paper wrappings and bit into the crab, shell and all, grinding the sharp spines down with his strong teeth. Still standing in the middle of the kitchen, he finished two of the clusters, shoving the pointy end of the last leg into his mouth as Elise entered.

Her eyes fell on the crab in his hand, then dropped to the shell remnants on the floor, gasping. "What are you doing?"

Caspian held out his hand, offering her the last cluster, which he had purposefully saved for her meal. "You said whatever I need is mine, and I needed nourishment." When she blinked at him in disbelief rather than accepting his gift, Caspian curled his fist around it and let his arm drop to his side. He'd done something wrong, something suspicious, though he wasn't sure what offense.

"That was supposed to be my birthday dinner." Elise flipped a curtain of wavy hair away from her eyes and stepped to a closet, where she retrieved a broom and used it to sweep up the uncomfortable crunchy pieces from the floor beneath his feet. "Do you always eat expensive seafood for breakfast?"

"I am sorry." He stepped out of the way, searching for a way to make right his misstep. A blush-colored sleep covering fluttered over smooth, golden skin, shielding her only from shoulder to thigh, and leaving arms and legs and feet and far too much human skin exposed. That skin stretched taught as she bent to scoop up the mess he'd left, reviving the desire that had engulfed him the night before. A desire he was only beginning to understand.

"It's all right, I guess." She stood and dumped the shells in the trash, and then leaned over the sink and pulled a cord. Light streamed in behind her, turning her hair to fire that would rival the crimson ball of sun in the sky.

As if realizing that he was looking, Elise folded her arms across her chest, sighing heavily. "Caspian, I'm trying hard to understand you, but it's obvious your culture is very different from mine."

He approached her slowly, refusing to remove his gaze from her face, longing to tell her, a virtual stranger, everything. More than everything, and knowing he could not. "Yes. We are indeed from different worlds."

46

Her eyelashes brushed her cheeks as she turned her face to the side, casting one half in shadow and the other with the truest, purest light. "I have to work again today, and I'm not . . . I'm not sure what to do with you, exactly. I'm not sure I want to leave you here without knowing . . ."

Without realizing it, he'd closed the distance between them and had boxed her against the counter. Tiny bumps rose along her skin, spreading across her shoulders and down both arms. Caspian reminded himself, more forcefully, that acting on his desire would bring shame to them both—but he craved to taste those plump lips and know the difference between human and Mer. To explore more of her than he currently saw, to fully experience a human female who might soon disappear from his life forever.

Determined to preserve Elise's honor, he inched back, reaching his hand to hers and bringing it toward him, palm up, so he could place the last crab cluster in it. "For you."

She stared at the crab, bright blue eyes blinking at it, then at him, holding him hostage with their intensity. Blink. Blink. Blink.

Shaking herself out of her trance, she set the crab aside. "You might as well eat it. No point in cooking it now." She glibly stepped around him, keeping her eyes cast anywhere but on him. "I'm going to take a shower.

I guess you're coming with me to work, unless you'd rather I drop you at the mental facility."

Clutching the edge of the counter, and staring at the gift she'd refused, Caspian forced a smile he didn't feel. "I would quite enjoy another burger."

Chapter Six

"I THOUGHT YOU WERE TAKING him to a hospital."
Marcus fed chunks of meat into the grinder and then
added his special blend of spices into the mixer as the
ground beef plopped out the other end. "He's not
stable, Elise. We all saw proof of that yesterday. I can't
believe you took a stranger—a mental one—into your
house. Where you live alone. Your father would shit
blocks if he was still alive."

Elise set a flatware place setting on top of a linen
napkin and rolled it into a decorative bundle in
preparation for the lunch rush. "I couldn't do it,
Marcus. I know it sounds crazy, but there's something
about him—I just don't feel like he's the type that
would do well locked up."

"Type? There's no such thing a type when it comes
to mental health. He has problems. Big ones." Marcus

fired up the grill to get it preheating while he sectioned the meat into balls, and then pounded each ball into a patty. "They're more likely to medicate him than lock him up. Maybe put him into some type of therapy. I don't know. Doesn't matter what the treatment is, Elise. It's *not* spending an indefinite amount of time living in your house. He's a stranger."

"When you put it that way, *I* sound like the crazy one." She stepped away from the counter and cracked open the swinging door to peek at Caspian. She'd returned him to the same corner booth as yesterday, where he now fiddled with sugar packets, lifting them in the air, and then dropping them on the table, delighted each time they fell. *Odd duck.* She returned to her task. "I want to help him find his mother, or his home—whatever he's looking for. Maybe his mental block is temporary. He's probably experienced some sort of trauma, and his brain has blocked it as a coping mechanism. It happens sometimes."

Marcus lined up a row of patties on a tray, pressing them down with the flat of his spatula, then started another. "Not in a stranger's house, sleeping in a stranger's room and wearing that stranger's clothes. Sounds like enabling, to me."

A lock of hair skimmed across Elise's eyes, and she blew it away with a strong huff. "He has no clothes with him, except the ones he had on yesterday. I had to loan him my father's, because mine would never in a million years fit. He's at least twice my size, if not three-times."

"Exactly why I'm worried." Marcus whirled on Elise, sparks flashing in his eyes. "At least tell me you slept with the door locked and your phone in your hand."

"I'm not stupid. I sleep like that every night, especially when I'm alone." Except the phone part—she hadn't told him it was turned off.

Knowing there was no way she could explain that she somehow knew—by instinct or something stronger—that Caspian would never hurt her, Elise piled the napkin bundles onto her tray until she had enough to set the tables. It had been a relief to have someone else under her roof, to know that she wasn't as completely alone as usual. She wasn't lying to Marcus. She'd spent her childhood afraid of the dark, and now she spent her nights alone, door locked, lifeless phone under her pillow, and her father's gun in the nightstand drawer. Just in case.

"At least tell me you're taking him to the hospital today." Marcus covered the tray and set it on a shelf in the fridge, then got to work on more patties. "You can't just let him move in with you. He's a stranger, who we know literally nothing about. And you can't afford to feed an extra person who isn't capable of holding a job."

Elise pulled the edge of the tray into her stomach and backed against the swinging door that led into the dining room. "Maybe you should give me more hours, then." She let the door swing closed on Marcus's objection, and bustled around the room placing the designated number of flatware on each table. When she arrived at Caspian's, she slid onto the seat across from him, the same way she had the previous day. "Whatcha doin?"

Caspian opened his palm to reveal a fist full of pink sugar packets, then tipped his hand so they dropped, one at a time, onto the table. "These stones have a fascinating scent, and they react to gravity so quickly. I cannot recall ever having seen something so small drop so quickly."

Elise picked up one of the packets, choking back a laugh. "It's just sugar." She held one by the corner, and ripped a whole side off a packet, showing him the white granules inside. "Like, for coffee or cereal."

He stared into the packet. "I do not know what is coffee, but I know cereal from before, when I was small and lived with Mother." As if memory struck him in the head, he snatched the packet from Elise and dumped it into his mouth so fast that the dry sugar traveling down his throat triggered a coughing attack.

Trying not to laugh at how Caspian's childish glee turned self-destructive, Elise stood to retrieve the fresh pot of coffee and two mugs. She set one in front of Caspian, and filled it with steaming black liquid. Immediately, he wrapped his long fingers around it, gasping when a drop of hot coffee sloshed onto his hand, leaving an angry, red welt. "I have not yet tasted this drink, and already find it not to my liking. Liquid should not be hot."

Elise remained standing, but filled her own cup so she could show Caspian how to add milk and sugar before he burned his tongue and throat. "Sip slowly, or you'll be sorry."

He took the first sip, nose wrinkling and mouth puckering with distaste. "Nope. Not to my liking."

She added another packet of sugar and stirred it in, then set the spoon aside, glancing at the door to the kitchen as Marcus called her name.

"Elise, what's taking you? Doors open in ten minutes and we're nowhere near ready."

"I'm coming." She sighed, wishing—for the first time in months—that she could skip out on work and spend the day at the beach with Caspian. He wrapped his hands around the cup again, so she covered the top with her hand, fingers resting on his and sending tingles into her toes. "Don't drink it yet. Let it cool first, then try it."

"Elise, we don't have all day." Marcus bellowed, increasingly demanding.

Caspian peered toward the kitchen, but made no move to disconnect the touch. "He sounds angry. I do not wish to cause you trouble."

I think it's too late for that. Elise's head spun with giddy pleasure, just from being near him, and she had to work hard to avoid behaving like a fifteen-year-old going on her first date. "Look, you don't have to stay here all day." She aimed a thumb over her shoulder, indicating the beach they could see out the window. "There's a towel in my trunk. You can lie on the beach while you wait. Just don't wander too far away, or I won't be able to find you."

He set the cup aside and turned his hand over so that their palms pressed together. "But *I* will find *you*, no matter how far I wander. You are as glowing plankton, lighting up the sea."

Struck mute by Caspian's sweet words, Elise withdrew her hand and started for the kitchen. Yep. It was far too late to avoid trouble.

She wasn't sure when he left the café, but anxiety pooled in her chest, starting from the moment she noticed him gone. *He'll be back,* she told herself. *He's not your responsibility anyway.* But given his level of confusion, Elise worried in the same way she would have worried about any friend who wasn't doing well.

There was no way for her to know how long he'd been suffering from whatever afflicted his mind, but she'd noticed a marked improvement from the time she'd first found him until she'd left him sitting alone in that booth this morning. His recognition of small, everyday customs seemed to be returning, and she couldn't help but feel like he would continue to improve as long as she watched over him. Multiple times during her shift, she caught herself distracted, watching through the window and searching for him in the crowd of summer sunbathers, nerves tightening her shoulders. Unfortunately, the crowds were too thick, or the window glass too smudged, or . . . he simply wasn't there.

"Excuse me, ma'am." A customer waved her over, grouchiness crinkling around his eyes as she returned to his table with her tray half full of entrees, waiting to be delivered. "Is that the rest of our order?"

She glanced at her current load, then at the ticket, realizing that she'd set down two of their five plates, and then left with the rest still on her tray. If her hands had been free, she would have hidden her face behind them. As it was, blood rose into her cheeks, burning along the tips of her ears. "I'm so sorry. I don't know what's wrong with me." She delivered the remainder, continuing to apologize as she made sure that they didn't need anything else, and then fled to the hallway off the kitchen, where she set her tray down on a shelf and leaned against the wall, closing her eyes and taking a calming breath.

"You okay?" Shelley skirted around Elise to pluck her apron off the hook and stow her purse in one of six square lockers meant for the staff.

Elise opened her eyes, exhaustion seeping from every pore. She couldn't remember the last time work had drained more energy than it gave her. "I'm great. Why?"

Shelly tied the apron around her waist, removing a lipstick from the pocket and shifting so she could see herself in the pocket-sized mirror she'd stuck to her locker door. "Marcus says you're having an off day."

When Elise initially awoke that morning, she heard movement in her kitchen and knew that she wasn't alone. Since the moment she'd met him, childlike innocence shone in Caspian's eyes, delivered in his words, even as he stood unashamedly naked in the bathroom doorway—offering her his salt-encrusted clothes—nothing about him had given her reason to feel threatened, regardless of her inexplicable temptation to be near him.

Even when she'd caught him eating the expensive crab legs—set aside for a special occasion—she still couldn't regret having brought him home, rather than to a hospital.

He needed her, and it had been a long time since Elise had felt needed by anyone.

"I'm just tired," she told Shelley. "Can't remember the last time I had a day off. Long before Becca quit and Justice left for her trip."

"You're definitely due for at least a day. Maybe a month, even." Shelley finished applying the lipstick, pressing her lips together, and then blotting with a tissue. She rolled perfume on her wrists and neck, convinced that both efforts gained her larger, more significant tips. "You should tell Marcus you want to go home early." She snapped on a watch and checked the time against her cell phone. "Maggie will be here in an hour, and we can probably handle the dinner rush without you."

Evenings were their busiest time at the Turtle, so staying would mean she left at the end of the night with a pocketful of tips, but worry for Caspian drove her to consider something she'd never done before—something she'd never expected herself to do. She shuffled into the kitchen and told Marcus that she wasn't feeling well, knowing he would send her home to avoid having her contaminate anyone's food.

When she hadn't seen Caspian by the time Maggie arrived, Elise's feigned illness was no longer a flat-out lie, because her stomach had tied itself into knots. She hoped he hadn't gotten lost, or into trouble, or worse—had some sort of accident—but considering his instability, any option could be reality.

She removed her company apron and retrieved her belongings, then poked her head into the kitchen to tell Marcus thanks. "Don't thank me yet," he scolded. "If the new girl can't handle the volume, I might have to call you back in, just to save face with the regulars."

Why is it always on me to take the hardest shifts? "I'm sure she'll do fine. She's already doing better than me today, and that says a lot about her progress. And now you have Maggie. She tolerates even fewer mistakes than I do."

Marcus handed Elise a paper carryout bag filled with food, grease-stains already dotting the front. "Dinner to go, for you and your friend. Noticed you're getting thin, lately."

His eyes flicked to the shorts that hung baggy around her waist, informing her, in no uncertain terms, that he'd been paying attention. Actions like this were the reason Elise chose to work for Marcus in the first place, and would have, even if he hadn't been friends with her father. She stretched onto her toes and kissed his cheek. "Thank you. I promise, I'll try harder."

She started for the door, but Marcus called out to her. "I'll be stopping by your place after close. Want to check in and make sure you're still feeling safe around this guy. If not, he's out. Period, no arguing. Got it?"

"Got it," she called, having ignored most of his words as she pushed through the door and into the bright, summertime sun. She glanced up and down the beach, then blindly picked a direction and started walking.

Chapter Seven

AFTER SPENDING THE AFTERNOON DIGGING his feet into the sand and letting the water lap at his ankles, Caspian decided that he had successfully figured out this walking thing. Though he'd felt wobbly the first few times, by now he'd covered a significant amount of ground, searching every face, every laugh, every voice, for the mother he'd come here to find.

He'd traveled too far to keep the diner in his view, so when the sun dipped toward the blue ocean horizon, and the beach-combers thinned out, he turned around and headed back, longing for another moment with Elise.

Lodging in her home had not been part of his plan. He would not have been bothered to sleep in the cave where he'd first emerged, and forage for his food, but when Elise invited him into her home, his subconscious had begun to form new ideas. Forbidden ones. He should swim away, as leaving was perhaps the only way to avoid becoming attached to another human he would eventually be forced to leave. But he simply couldn't depart from her. Not yet.

Every time he thought of Elise—which was pretty much nonstop—his entire being begged him to return to her. He convinced himself that the draw was caused by curiosity. Human females had proven different from the mermaids he'd grown up with, and that must surely be the reason for his longing. He *was* here to find his mother—but until then, he intended to know more of Elise. Perhaps human rules were not the same as those established for the Mer. Perhaps once he touched her, tasted her, he would stop thinking of her in such forbidden ways.

A child ran screaming into the water, cutting off Caspian's steady stride, and a mother chased the boy, scolding him for running away. Distracted by the child's squealing, and brain filled with thoughts of Elise, Caspian failed to notice the female beckoning him from far out in the sea, until the mother screamed, shouting about a woman who was drowning. Caspian turned, focusing on the figure in the distance. Annoyance prickled when he realized that Marietta had broken a very important law by showing herself to the humans. Now, he was obligated to protect her from being locked in the palace dungeons, not to mention protecting himself from falling under the scrutiny of the humans.

The mother continued to scream as Marietta moved closer to the shore, which Caspian knew would only cause more trouble. Desperate to escape the shouting, Caspian waded until the water covered his thighs, and then he dove, far, and long, and fast, reaching Marietta far more quickly than should have been humanly possible.

She ducked below the surface, beckoning for him to follow, but Caspian refused, surfacing again, as his gills had been temporarily sealed. Marietta rose to meet him. "What are you doing at the surface?" he asked, unable to hide how his hands sparked with electric fury.

"I have come to bring you home," she said. "You have found your mother, and now it is time to return so that we might be joined."

Caspian shook water out of his eyes, surprised to find that the salt had irritated them as never before. "I have *not* found my mother. There are many humans on land, and I do not remember the location of her dwelling." Marietta moved toward him, so he backed away in defense. "I am not ready for joining, Marietta. That is why I have come to land."

Sparks flashed in Marietta's eyes, and haunting melody accompanied her next words. "You are running out of time, Caspian. We must be joined soon. Return with me."

He stuck his face into the water again, keeping his eyes open and inviting the burn. Replying to Marietta's statement took several seconds longer than it should have, since Caspian had to force his brain to connect with his words, rather than simply doing as she commanded. Many of the Mer had been blessed with this influential ability, and Marietta was one of them. Yet another reason why he did not wish to join with her—her strong-willed aspirations could generate a negative impact on all of Atlantis.

Finally, he managed to find his voice. "I will take what time I need. I must first find my mother." And, he decided, thinking of Elise, experience the taste of a human woman's mouth. Surely tasting her mouth would not cause her shame?

"I will not wait forever." Marietta's fingers rose from the water with long, pointed nails and raked through her wild mane of lavender hair. "I am of noble blood, and desired by many. If you do not honor your father's wishes, I will find another noble with whom to join. Atlantis will be left without an heir."

Though he knew it was an empty threat—Marietta wanted the throne far worse than Caspian ever had—the idea that she would seek another mate further fueled his desire to avoid returning, and solidified his resolve to spend more time with Elise. "If that is your wish, I give you freedom to make that choice." He glanced at the shore, where the woman still stood, holding the hand of her child, waving for them to come back before they drowned. "You must go. I shall return to shore and deal with the humans. Do not return here, Marietta. In doing so, you have put all Mer in danger. This is law, and when my father learns you have broken it, he will punish you according to my will."

"He will not punish me when I am Queen." Electricity sparked in her fingers. "Do not keep me waiting, Caspian. Or I will return, and expose you to the humans that fascinate you so." She dove below, deliberately swishing her fin above for a giant splash that sent Caspian hurtling toward the shore.

Anger fueled him as he cut through the waves, frustrated at the clothing that weighed him down. He stood in waist-high water, waving at the anxious mother who seemed anxious to hear what had happened. "A dolphin was caught in fishing nets. I freed it, and it swam away. All is well."

The human picked up her child and balanced him on her hip. "No, that was a woman. I swear it was. I saw her face."

Caspian turned his back on her. "You are mistaken. If there was a human in the sea, I would not have left her to drown. A dolphin, only. Struggling and afraid, but still a dolphin."

Leaving the humans behind, Caspian picked up his pace, more eager than ever to return to The Sea Turtle and Elise.

By the time he spotted the café in the distance, the horizon glowed warm pink, and the last sunrays stretched as skeins of diamonds across the water. Golden sand sparkled as mother of pearl, dazzling his eyes and filling his thoughts with ideas. He loved his life in Atlantis. As a Prince, he held the respect and admiration of all the city, was privy to inside knowledge, and had the ability to make governing decisions that would further bring peace and justice among the Mer. In coming ashore, he had only intended to visit his mother, to know of her whereabouts and discover the origins of his human heritage. But Marietta's mention of choice, of the possibility of joining with another, had planted the seed of an idea that Caspian had not yet considered.

If he chose, he could live as a human, join with a human, and still produce an heir to Atlantis. Perhaps his fate hadn't been decided for him, as he'd come to believe.

Down the beach, a figure advanced, calling his name. Caspian shaded his eyes with a hand against his forehead. "Elise?"

Remembering his impure thoughts from only moments ago, and the ones he'd wrestled during the night, shyness overcame him, rooting his feet into the sand. Oblivious to his newfound nerves, Elise threw her arms around him, squeezing tight. "I thought you were lost. I was so worried."

When she didn't let go, Caspian wrapped his arms around her as well, heart racing as the action caused her body to press tight against his, in a fashion that fitted their two shadows into one. "I am sorry you worried. I did not believe I was gone long."

"Hours," she insisted. "You've been gone for hours."

He had noticed that humans measured time differently from the Mer, but he could not explain to Elise why the difference confused him. "I am sorry. I did not realize. It was not my intention to worry you."

She took a shaky breath, finally letting go of him and replacing her feet on the hot sand. "I would never forgive myself if something happened to you. Marcus keeps telling me that I should take you to a hospital, and if you'd been lost, I would have known he's right, and that you being lost was *my* fault. He's probably right anyway."

Alarm stole Caspian's breath. "I do not wish to visit a hospital. I must find my mother first."

She bent to catch a shell as a wave turned it end over end, dragging it out to sea. "You keep saying that, but I'm not sure it's possible. Without a name, or a phone number or address—there's not a lot we can do to search."

He thought of the tablet on which Maui had written the human symbols. Perhaps Elise would know what to do with such information, but showing her would also mean explaining where this information had come from, where he had come from, and his father's warning echoed in his mind again. He could not bear the idea of Elise being torn apart by sharks, or otherwise targeted by his powerful father. And by now, he was certain that the memories he had left of his mother had taken place on this specific stretch of beach. "My mother will come to me."

Elise stopped, blinking against the bright light. "Depending on how old she is, she might not be able to. Does she even know you're here? That you're looking for her?"

Blood pumped into his cheeks, a sensation Caspian didn't entirely hate, as it wasn't something he ever experienced underwater. "She does not know. But she will visit this beach. When I was a child, we visited nightly. She will always visit this place."

Elise took his hand, clasping it between both of hers as she faced him. "That day we met at the cemetery, were you looking for your mother's grave, as I believed?"

"No." His hand tingled where she touched him, reminding him of how it had felt to have her body pressed against his, how well they fit together. "I was simply lost."

A sigh of relief caused her chest to rise and fall. "Are you looking for your mother because you were adopted? Is that why you don't know her name?"

Adopted? He didn't know what this word meant, but he did not want to lie to Elise, any more than he wanted to tell her the truth, so he settled in the middle, giving only as much truth as he dared. "I was raised by my father in a place far away. I have not seen my mother since I was very small, and I do not remember many things about our life here. But I wish to find her, before I am to be joined."

She dropped his hand as if burned by the electrical current he was known to emit below the sea. "Joined. As in married? Caspian, are you engaged?"

Her reaction, coupled with the look on her face, gave him cause to choose his words carefully. "Only if my father has his way. I do not chose to be with my betrothed, but if I am to return home, it will not be my choice."

"I see." Her back stiffened as if she did see, but the muscles in her jaw relaxed, her smile returning. "So, you ran away."

"Yes. To find my mother and seek her counsel."

Her smile grew into a grin. "All this time, I've thought your brain was broken, that you'd snapped. But I was wrong. You're not crazy, you're just confused and emotionally . . . frustrated."

The sparkle had returned to her eyes, and Caspian could not help but match her grin with one of his own. "Correct. I do not need a hospital, or a healer, Elise. I need only to find my mother and escape a union I did not request, and to which I am opposed."

She took his hand again, this time, threading it through her own as she drew him down the beach. "I might not be able to help find your mother right now, but the escape part I think I can manage. Come with me."

Chapter Eight

SINCE CASPIAN HAD GONE SWIMMING in his clothes again, Elise took him home to clean him up. While he showered, she picked out another set of her father's clothes, only this time, once the bathroom door was closed, she remained silent about washing the ones he had on.

He was such a peculiar, interesting man, and having him near stirred something inside her that she'd once believed long gone. Whether she liked it or not, she had begun to care for Caspian. She cared about his physical well-being, and what was going on in his head, and especially his emotional state. Loneliness gave her a strong insight into the needs of others, and she felt a great deal of need coming from him.

When he emerged from the bathroom, he'd wrapped a towel around his waist, but his soaked hair dripped in rivers, water bending around the curves of each muscle as it flowed down his back and into the towel. Again, he had wadded his clothes into a tight bundle, which he handed to Elise. "Thank you for providing me with suitable coverings. I remember very little from my childhood, but I have seen that the customs in this land require many body parts to be hidden."

His brow furrowed in such concentrated confusion, that a giggle bubbled in Elise's chest, and she had to press her lips together to hold it in. "Yes, that's true. There are laws against public nudity. You could be put in jail if you're not careful."

His eyes widened in horror, and the fist holding up his towel tightened. "I was not aware of such laws. I hope you would not have me locked up for showing myself to you before."

The giggle escaped, despite her best efforts. "Don't worry. The only laws about nudity in private homes are the ones that . . ." She paused, realizing that trying to explain would only confuse him further. "It's okay to show yourself at home, as long as the people who also live there don't mind."

"That is a relief." His shoulder muscles visibly relaxed, and he dropped the towel, startling a squeak from Elise, who instinctively covered her eyes.

"Okay. Caspian, look. I understand that you're confused as hell right now, especially because walking around naked is apparently no big deal where you're from. But, um." She opened her eyes and peered through the crack between her fingers, cursing herself, and the curiosity that drove her to look. "We don't know each other *that* well yet, okay? I'd feel more comfortable if you covered up. At least, for now."

Confusion paraded across his face as he picked up the towel and draped it around his toned, tapered waist, holding it there with one strong hand. "I am covered," he said. "There is no longer a need to protect your eyes."

She dropped her hand, forcing herself to keep her attention on his face, rather than be distracted by what seemed like miles and miles of rippled muscles. "Thank you. I know that most women wouldn't be bothered by having a man walk around naked in their homes, but I'm . . . I . . ." How could she tell him that she'd never seen a naked man in person before? That she'd never experienced the thing so many of her friends had been doing for years? Not because she hadn't had the desire. There simply had never been someone who meant enough to her. There had never been a man she had trusted with her heart, or her body.

She picked up the clean clothes and offered them to him. "I just need some time, is all."

He accepted the garments with a nod. "Mixing cultures can be confusing. This is something I know well." Clothes folded against his chest, he returned to the bathroom, and Elise let out a breath of relief.

She stood on the most dangerous of grounds when it came to Caspian, especially considering that he was one half of an arranged marriage, somewhere far away. The undeniable draw she felt toward him could not be dismissed as mere physical attraction. Not when being near him felt so familiar and fulfilling. Especially when she'd only known him for two days, but had spent the previous night dreaming of a future that included the two of them together.

She plopped onto the couch, arm crossed over her face to block out the light, and let out a giant sigh. "He's not staying here forever," she reminded herself. "Probably can't. Don't let him break your heart in the meantime."

With all the uncertainties that came from having a virtual stranger stay in her house, Elise experienced an unusual surge of bravery. She'd never been one for going to clubs or spending her evenings at bars, especially since she usually worked. But every night on her way home, she passed a beach-bar night club, located only half a block from The Sea Turtle. She'd been curious about the place since it had opened last summer, and decided tonight would be a good time to take Caspian, and check it out.

After changing into a gauzy sundress that had the slightest hint of shimmer woven through the fabric, she pinned her hair up and applied mascara and lip gloss— both of which made her feel ultra-feminine, one step closer to sexy. She convinced herself that she wasn't dressing up for Caspian, that it was about enjoying a rare occasion, but there was no denying the flood of satisfaction she received when he did a double take upon seeing her.

His mouth worked like a fish as he searched for words, and his hands clenched and unclenched at his sides. "Are we to attend an event?"

Elise felt her lips curve into a sultry smile as she picked up her purse and keys, and led Caspian outside. "Not any particular event. I just thought we could go somewhere different—do something fun—while you're staying with me." She locked the front door, then turned to Caspian, who continued to stare. "Is that all right with you? Or would you rather stay home and watch TV?"

He licked his lips, tearing his eyes away from the curve-hugging dress so he could focus on her face, only to have them land on her glossy mouth. "I do not know what is TV, but I am happy to go anywhere, so long as I am with you."

Though she'd determined to keep things simple between them, the hunger in his eyes re-affirmed their mutual attraction, stirring within her a reckless streak. She trailed a finger along his arm, then crooked it, summoning him to follow. "Well, then. Let's go."

Cars lined the road leading to the lot, and then continued past for as far down the street as she could see. People clustered near the door, leaving Elise worried that they may have to wait to get in. She pulled into the lot anyway, feeling exceptionally lucky when an SUV backed out, freeing a prime spot near the exit.

As they approached the building, Caspian fidgeted with his necklace, lips pressed together and eyes darting from stranger to stranger, as the crowd flowed from the outside-in.

Elise stopped him with a hand on his bicep. "Are you okay? We don't have to go inside if you're too nervous."

He blinked, visibly loosening the tightness in his jaw. "I will be fine. It is only that I have never been around so many humans at once, and I am uncertain how one is expected to behave in this place."

"I understand. I'm not big on crowds either." She skimmed her hand down his arm and tangled their fingers together, squeezing tight. "Just hold onto me, and we'll figure it out together."

He pulled her closer into his side. "I believe that I will enjoy myself in any situation, so long as you are near."

Electrical currents zinged through her skin, starting from where their palms pressed together, and branching out to every long-forgotten muscle and nerve. Courage crashed into Elise in ways it never had before, and even though she had accepted that Caspian would only be a temporary fixture in her life, she decided against continuing to fight a losing battle over her natural urges. If all they ever had together was tonight, they might as well make it one neither of them would soon forget.

She dragged him inside, heading straight for the bar, where she ordered two sodas, and then led Caspian to a standing table, far in the back, where dancefloor and sand met. He held tight to her fingers, his eyes growing round and astonished when a live keyed up a fast-paced tune.

"Do you want to dance?" She set their sodas on the table and dragged Caspian onto the rough wooden floor, the beat thrumming in her chest along with the rhythm of her heart.

He didn't object, but when they got to the dancefloor, stood studying Elise as her body flowed, fluid with the pulse of lights and sound. When he didn't even try, Elise stood on tiptoes to speak into his ear. "Do you not know how? It's okay. Just do what I do."

She settled her hands on his shoulders and shook her hips, swaying their bodies with smooth control. When he caught onto that, she added a step to one side, back, then the other side. Once he had that down, she removed her hands, reluctantly, and added movement in her upper body, which he mimicked. Before long, they were both pink and sweating from exertion, and laughing with the delight as they returned to their table.

Caspian downed his drink in two gulps, gasping after he swallowed as if he'd forgotten how to breathe.

"Are you okay?" Elise wiped sweat from the side of his face with a napkin.

He grinned, wrapping his fingers around her wrist. "I am wonderful. More than wonderful. I very much enjoy this thing you call dancing. It is almost like swimming, only in the air."

Her smile hitched. It was the second time tonight that his wording formed a cloud of wariness in her brain. No matter what country a person came from, she was certain customs from every culture included some sort of dancing.

He let go of her wrist, rattling the ice in his glass. "I am going to get us more drinks."

She nodded, needing a moment to catch her breath anyway, and turned her face toward the sea breeze. She'd believed him when he told her that he wasn't crazy, but now a new theory began to form. What if he'd been kidnapped and held captive for most of his life? She certainly hoped not, but he seemed so confused about the simplest things. How damaging would something like that be to a man's emotions? His mental state?

He returned carrying drinks of a different variety. Frozen white, with swirls of pink and blue and topped with an umbrella and a cherry.

"What is it?" Elise sipped, surprised to find the sweetness tempered by a pleasant tang.

"I do not know." He gestured vaguely at the bar. "I took them from the serving platform."

Elise set her drink on the table, eyes wide. "Did you order them?"

He shook his head. "I did not need to. They appeared in front of me as I approached. In my home, it is not uncommon for the server to decide what must be offered at an event."

Laughing, Elise buried her face in her hands. "Oh dear. You took someone else's drinks? Did you pay for them?"

He blinked, his cheeks flushing. "Pay? With gold? I did not. But I am happy to do so."

A glance at the bar assured her that the drinks had not been missed yet—or if they had, the bartender had already forgotten them and made new ones. She let go of her concerns and nestled closer to Caspian, sipping on the frosty concoction and feeling light-headed from his nearness.

The music slowed, the tempo shifting into something dreamy and sweet, and once they'd emptied their cocktails—which may, or may not have been spiked—Elise drew Caspian back to the dance floor, winding her arms around his neck and fitting their bodies together as they moved.

Every place where his skin touched hers flared to life, each pulse in his veins thrumming in time to hers, each of his breaths that brushed her ear, her hair, her bare neck, sent shivers of awareness screaming to her core.

He had scars. Two long, thin lines on either side of his neck. She made a mental note to ask him about them later, but for now, ran her lips lightly over the one nearest to her face. Goosebumps raised on his skin, and his rhythm faltered. Power flowed into Elise—a boldness she had never felt as she pressed her lips more firmly to his neck and laid a trail of kisses behind his ear.

"Elise," he whispered, his voice strained. "I am not experienced in such things. I do not wish to bring dishonor to you, or to your future mate."

The sweetness of his concern only fueled her desire, enflaming her determination to leave this night with no regrets. "I'm not experienced either," she admitted. "I've never met someone who tempted me the way you do."

"Temptation causes heartache when acted upon."

Elise grinned, crushing her body against his, as she'd done when she'd hugged him on the beach. "Do I tempt you, Caspian?"

A tremor shook him, and his arms squeezed tighter around her waist. "I have never wanted *any* female in all the ways that I want you at this moment."

Her inhibitions broke free, setting loose the recklessness she'd always known lurked beneath her thick layers of reason. "I'm not afraid of heartache," she whispered, lips against his ear, nibbling his lobe. "But I am afraid of regret. I don't ever want to regret my experience with you—nor do I want you to regret yours with me."

While she focused on Caspian's skin beneath her lips, Caspian steered them off the dancefloor and onto the sand, yards away from the pulsing crowd and the lights, strung in rows above the revelry. They were not hidden in complete darkness, but had stepped far away from the limelight of the club, shielded by shadows from the prying eyes of drunken vacationers.

Caspian cradled her face between his hands, his eyes piercing hers in that gentle way that had first caused her to trust him—long before she invited him into her car, her work, her home, her heart. "I will never, ever regret my time with you, Elise. If I never find my mother, if I am forced to return home without the resolutions I've sought, my time here will have been well spent, because I have been with you." He closed the distance between their lips, pressing his to hers in the most innocent, sweet responsiveness she'd ever experienced with a boy—no, a man.

Sensations rocketed through her body as she took the kiss deeper, opening her mouth and her soul, offering him everything she was, and everything she had. When their tongues tangled, heat exploded in her core, leaving her more breathless than the dancing. Caspian tore his mouth from hers and pressed their foreheads together. "Elise, please understand . . ."

"I know." She nodded, refusing to hear reminders of how short his time would be, refusing to consider the woman who was supposed to become his wife, refusing to consider the consequences of what they were about to do. "No regrets, remember?"

He kissed her again, dragging her further from the light, toward a nearby beach resort, where a number of permanent structures had been fenced off to keep intruders out. "You must promise me," he said again. "Promise you will not wish me from your memory. Promise you will not curse me when I'm gone."

The cloud of concern she'd felt earlier nudged her, but was obliterated when his hand crept down the back of her dress and pulled her tighter against his body. "I'll promise you, if you promise me."

He broke away and took her hand, dragging her toward a covered cabana, and an outdoor swing bed surrounded by tied-back curtains. When an iron fence blocked their entry, Caspian grabbed hold of the locked gate and rattled it until it sparked, and then swung open. "How did you do that?" she asked.

Without answering, he led her through the gate and swung it closed again, leaving them alone in a darkness broken only by the light of a half-moon. "I promise," he said, his lips seeking hers again. "I will treasure us, for always."

"Me too. I will too." When he wrapped his arms around her back and tipped her toward the bed, she didn't resist, deciding instead to let everything happen the way she'd always hoped it would.

Chapter Nine

FOR TWO FULL WEEKS, CASPIAN and Elise remained inseparable. Every day, they woke up tangled together in her bed, had breakfast together, and experienced the intimacy of a daily routine, which sometimes included sharing the shower. Each day, when Elise left for work, Caspian came with her, and while she waited tables, he looked for his mother.

"You're in a good mood this morning." Shelley peered at Elise as she tied on her apron, unconsciously humming a song she and Caspian had danced to that night at the club. "In fact, you've been quite chipper all week."

Though her cheeks warmed, Elise reminded herself of her no-regrets promise, and decided that meant no embarrassment, either. But that didn't mean she was ready to talk about it. What she shared with Caspian felt solid and true, though she knew the reality was far from either of those things. Fragile and temporary, a road ending in certain heartbreak for them both. Until then, she refused to discuss the details with anyone, and instead kept her happiness to herself, hoping to store up enough to help her survive when he left.

"The sun's shining, the water's blue, and my tips this week have been exceptional. Good enough reasons, don't you think?"

Shelley snorted. "You just keep telling yourself that, honey. I know a girl in love when I see one—been there way too many times myself." She tucked a lock of hair behind Elise's ear. "Just promise me you'll be careful about that one, okay? He's not right in the head. Not a good foundation for a long-term relationship."

"He's not crazy," Elise insisted for what felt like the hundredth time. "That was a misunderstanding."

Shelley sighed, concern coloring her voice. "Yet, he's still living at your house, wearing your father's clothes, eating food you provide, and paying nothing. I don't see him looking for a job, since he comes here with you every day. Then there's the way he talks. I don't know where he's from, but it's not here. Too many things just don't add up."

It took effort for Elise not to squirm. She'd had so many similar thoughts over the last weeks, but the few times she'd probed Caspian about one thing or another, he'd found a way to change the subject or otherwise distract her. But when he touched her, when he kissed her, when he loved her, all her doubts and questions disappeared, leaving only true, solid feelings in their wake.

"It's under control," she lied to her friend. "Don't worry about me, okay?"

Shelley grinned, putting away her lipstick and slamming her locker shut. "What kind of a friend would I be if I didn't worry?"

To that, Elise had no answer. Of all the friends she'd considered close while she was in school, none had seemed the least concerned when her life was flipped topsy-turvy. She had never felt more truly alone than she had this year. Until Caspian.

Marcus met her at the door between the dining room and kitchen. "I need to talk to you for a minute."

Elise followed him back, leaning against the counter while he chopped vegetables for his burger station. "Shelley already gave me the lecture about how worried you all are, so if this is another one of those, there's no need."

"Well, I'm glad Shelley did that, but no. That's not the thing. At least not today." He ran his sharp knife through a tomato, slicing with the quick, sure precision of a master chef. "Last night, about an hour after you left, a woman came in. She was asking about a man who she'd heard spends his days wandering the beach, looking for someone."

Her stomach tied into tiny sailor knots. What if this woman was Caspian's mother? What would he do when he found her and resolved whatever emotional issues he'd come here to deal with? *He'll leave*, she thought. *He'll go home and leave me here.* Anguish tensed her shoulders. "Did she say what she wanted?"

The question was rhetorical for Elise, a formality, really, since this was not the kind of coincidence that just *happened*.

"Thought he might be her long-lost son, or brother—something like that. Anyway, I remembered Caspian saying something about looking for his mother, so I figured the two might be related. Wanted to let you know."

Elise's mouth went bone dry, her heart racing with newfound fear. She snagged a water bottle from the fridge and gulped down half of it, and once she found her voice, asked, "Did she leave contact information?"

Marcus reached into his apron pocket and brought out a yellow sticky-note. "Name and phone number. Told her I'd have you call her if you saw him again."

He raised his eyebrows in question, though Elise wasn't sure why. Everyone knew Caspian was still staying at her house. They'd teased her about it relentlessly.

Swallowing a lump of nausea, she tucked the note into her pocket, doing her best to appear unconcerned as she headed into the dining room to prepare for the lunch rush. "Thanks. We'll check it out." Fear aside, Elise knew she had to tell Caspian, despite her hesitation.

But that night, when the two of them were finally alone, she found herself utterly distracted, and unable to bring up the subject. This happened the next night as well, and the next, until so many days had passed that Elise managed to shove the knowledge into the back of her mind and almost, almost forget about it.

Chapter Ten

IT WASN'T THAT HE'D STOPPED searching for his mother—he'd simply become consumed by life with Elise, and had unconsciously set his search aside. On his first days ashore, he'd tucked Maui's tablet into his pocket, determined to decipher what he now knew to be numbers, and make use of the information. But the morning after he'd first experienced the wonder that was Elise, he'd tucked the tablet between the mattresses in her father's bedroom, deciding that he might be better prepared if he were to come back to it later.

It was a lie of course, and he knew it even as he convinced himself otherwise. He'd avoided swimming, and stayed away from the areas where he knew the Mer might surface ever since. The full moon approached, and with it a reminder of his obligation to Marietta, so he avoided the beach by hiding in the resort where he'd first been intimate with Elise. Sometimes he walked along the road hoping to find fresh flowers he might pick for his beloved. He even spent a day allowing tourists to take pictures with him, since they perceived him as some variety of celebrity, with his rippled muscles and long, gleaming hair.

When a tourist tucked a green paper bill into Caspian's palm, he shoved it in his pocket, having seen the way Elise handled her tips—which she then used to buy food and pay for other needs. After that, he paid close attention to the green paper exchanging from person to person, studying the way it was treated as necessity—almost as important as the rectangular cards that appeared even more valuable than the green paper.

"Hey, man." Peter, one of the regular cabana boys, set a frosty drink on the side table next to Caspian's chair, and plopped onto an adjacent loveseat.

Caspian had pulled the curtains closed so no one would see who occupied the space, and he accepted the drink with a nod to his recently acquired friend. "Hello. Do you have need of this cabana today?"

He'd asked the same question for six days in a row, now, and Peter's response varied.

"Not today, my friend. You're lucky. Very few reservations mid-week mean that you're free to poach again."

"I thank you." Caspian tipped the glass to his mouth and drained half of it in two gulps. "Someday, I shall find a way to repay your kindness."

Peter propped his head on a pillow and kicked his feet onto the arm of the wicker loveseat, eyes closed. "I really hope so. If my boss ever decides to tally how many of those drinks I take away from the bar versus what people are paying for, I'm toast."

"Then you must stop bringing them to me." Caspian attempted to return the glass, via the hand Peter had dangling in the sand.

Peter popped an eye open, annoyed. "Dude. You can't poach a free cabana space all day and not drink. Should be against the law."

Caspian's eyes dropped to the sand, where his toes had burrowed below to find the cool, dampness beneath. "I do not know much of your laws here yet, but I can offer you this paper."

He dug into his pocket, producing several bills, which Peter immediately pocketed. "One of these days you're going to run out of that stuff and have to find a job. Can't live in an appropriated cabana forever, you know?"

He did know. With each day that he watched Elise wait tables, to the point of complete exhaustion, Caspian became increasingly aware of the human custom that required serving others in order to pay for their own basic needs. It bothered him to see his love struggle so hard.

Peter continued, "At some point, that girl of yours is going to get sick of working her ass off while you lounge on the beach, and she's going to kick you to the curb. Then what you gonna do?"

Caspian drained the remainder of his beverage, considering his options. "Might it be possible for me to also work?"

Peter laughed so hard he had to sit up, clutching his stomach. "Of course it's possible. Where are you from, anyway? Mars?"

"A land far away," Caspian replied, his standard response.

Peter waved off the explanation. "I know, I know. Anyway, point is, if you want to be a real man, you gotta work. At least contribute to family and society, even if you aren't planning on providing for them entirely."

Caspian considered the concept, having noticed how many humans—male and female—worked what Elise called *jobs* on this stretch of beach. "Where should I begin? And how?"

Peter replaced the pillow on the wicker sofa and fluffed it to look unused. "Where'd you get the money you just gave me? You have some significant bills, here. It's not small potatoes."

"From a tourist who wanted a picture. I do not know why."

Peter raised his eyebrows as if a brilliant idea had popped into his head. "Oh my . . . People must think you're a celebrity. You should capitalize on that. I'm going to suggest this to my manager, see if he'll hire you for special events. When you come back tomorrow, I'll let you know what he says. Bring your ID, just in case."

Making note of the angle of the sun, Caspian stood, offering a hand to Peter. "Thank you, my friend, Peter. I will return tomorrow, hoping for good news of a job."

As he returned to The Sea Turtle, Caspian's mind landed on Peter's mention of family, and how important his role should be in the world of humans. Though he'd avoided it for so long, he faced the water, staring past the horizon. Somewhere out there, miles below, his family continued living, thriving—ruling Atlantis. His father had inherited the grandest job available to any Mer, and this job would soon fall to Caspian.

He spun away from the sea, continuing his journey to the café where his beloved spent her days. He could not possibly obtain such a grand appointment ashore, but servant's work did not seem to bother Elise, thus, it should not bother Caspian, either.

Elise had also become like family, but to care for her in the way a merman should care for his mate, he would need to sever his ties to Atlantis and remain ashore forever. In this new land, he would be required to act as a servant, rather than the royal leader he could become at home.

Tempted though he was to consider staying ashore, having not found his mother yet came with a level of discouragement that caused mountains of doubt to form in his mind. Perhaps he had a duty to her as well, but if so, he was not fulfilling it by continuing to ignore his search. He had come ashore to find the woman who had given him life, but had instead become distracted by beauty and grace, as Maui had warned could happen.

None of this confusion was tempered by Peter's mention of something called ID, which Caspian felt certain he didn't have, and could not get without Elise's help. Perhaps it was time to tell her the thing from which he'd been protecting her. Now that he knew Elise rarely went near the water, he'd begun to doubt his father's threat of her being torn apart by sharks. Perhaps knowing his secret would hurt her in the beginning, as she had put so much faith in him. But if he were to tell her his true origins, and why he'd come, perhaps she could forgive him—with time. If she could not, maybe that would be his answer. He would be able to return to Atlantis, having loved, and lost, and lived during his time ashore, and become the better for it.

Yes, he thought. *I need to tell her.*

But the moment she burst through the door of the restaurant and threw herself into his arms, all thoughts of serious discussion fled his mind, and he focused instead on the sensation of touching her, of feeling her skin pressing against his, of tasting her mouth with the desire of the insatiable. He would tell her the truth someday. That day simply wouldn't be this one.

When Caspian arrived at the resort, Peter met him at the gate. "I'm glad you're here. My manager has some job openings and is interested in meeting you. Only problem is that once he does, you probably won't be able to poach our cabanas anymore during business hours, because he'll know you're not a member of the club or a vacationer."

But he would have something better to do. Something for which he might earn money that could help ease Elise's burdens. "What variety of job?"

Peter shrugged, gesturing for Caspian to follow as he started down the walk. "Ever carried drinks on a tray? Or food?"

Caspian's attention landed on a man in a white shirt, as he delivered an order to a couple sitting at a shaded table on the patio. "No, I have not."

"Know how to sell things in a gift shop? Are you talented with mechanical stuff? Or decent at cleaning?"

"I have never done any of those things." Caspian shook back his long hair. It had become increasingly frustrating to keep that hair from tangling in the sea breeze, or from flying every-which-way, regardless of his level of activity. Elise had suggested that he get it cut— but Caspian was not sure he'd know himself without his long mane.

Peter stopped, mid-step, whirling on Caspian. "Well, what *can* you do? I mean, besides looking pretty. Turns out, our manager only hires companies for photo ops, and since you don't work for a company, they won't touch you—something about a background check or whatever."

Squeals of delight echoed across the hot concrete, drawing Caspian's attention to the children's pool, complete with multiple water slides. "I can swim. Very well."

Peter grinned. "Excellent. Think you could pass a lifeguard test?"

Caspian indicated the young man standing at the pool's edge holding a floatation device. "To do what he does? Of course. I swim much faster than most humans."

"Okay then, that's what you apply for."

That evening, when he caught up with Elise outside The Sea Turtle, Caspian beamed with excitement when he took her in his arms and announced, "Elise, I have found a job."

She squeezed tight and kissed his neck before pulling away, surprise written in every inch of her expression. "A job? Here? I didn't realize you were looking."

The hope in her eyes urged him to be cautious. They'd become very attached to each other over the weeks, but he still could not commit to staying ashore forever. "I was not looking for a job, but I have made a friend at the resort, and he brought to my attention that they are seeking a guardian of life for the children's pool. I excel at swimming, and so I volunteered in exchange for funds."

The light of hope dimmed, ever-so-slightly, but she kept her smile in place. "Caspian, that's great news.

You'll make a terrific lifeguard. Does this mean you're planning to stay in Oceanside for a while?"

He draped his arm around her and steered her toward the car, anxious to get home where they could be alone once again. "I have not yet found my mother, and I cannot continue to allow you to care for me without compensation—"

"Wait, what?" Elise stopped, and all semblance of happiness or smiles disappeared from her face, from her very essence. "What do you mean by compensation?"

Confused, Caspian stuttered. "I . . . I only meant . . . My friend Peter suggested that a woman should not be expected to work every day in order to feed a man who does not *also* work. I have watched you at your job, and seen the strain it causes you. I wish to gain more of the green paper that is required to purchase food, that I might give it to you, and perhaps use some to bring you gifts."

She pressed her lips together, twisting a lock of her hair while she stared at him. "So, by compensation, you aren't talking about paying me for . . . anything else." A blush stained her cheeks the most becoming shade of peach.

"I do not understand what that means. I am only making an attempt to help provide funds, that you might have more time to spend at home, with me."

96

She let out a relieved breath, an embarrassed giggle attached. "There's a definite culture gap between us, and I have a tendency to forget about it until moments like this. You speak so formally."

Elise wound her fingers into his and completed the journey to the car, where she leaned against the driver's side door.

"I would like to speak as you do," he told her, realizing, as he said it, that it was true. Not only did he want to speak more like her, but part of him longed to live a simpler existence, in which he would be allowed to choose his path, rather than having it chosen for him. He'd learned so much about human customs, yet there was still much more to discover.

Elise's lashes swept up, her eyes pinning Caspian as she ran her hands up his chest and pulled him against her. "I like how different we are. Keeps things interesting." She reached behind him and tangled her fingers in his hair. "You even look exotic. I don't know anyone with hair this healthy and long, or skin so pale, or . . ." She squeezed his tight bicep with her free hand. "Who has muscles like these? They're insane."

Warmth bled into his cheeks as Caspian followed her lead, running his hand through her hair, as well, and marveling at its soft, fine texture. "I do not know a female such as you, either, my Elise. And I would not want to. You are as a lone pearl, harvested from a deep-water oyster—singular, and one of a kind, with color and light belonging only to you, and you alone."

"Where do you come up with these things?" she murmured, pressing her lips against his. "Do they teach classes on romance in your schools, or something? How could anyone possibly resist you?"

Though many days had passed since he'd swam in the sea, Maui's warning of the Mer pheromones lingered, always, behind his every thought. He did not wish for Elise to be caught in a chemical trap, but neither could he stay away. He'd stopped resisting the draw to be near her, and even now, could not get enough. "I am sure it's possible to resist me." He wrapped his fingers around the mane of her hair and tugged until he had full access to her slender, golden neck. "But I hope not for you." He pressed a kiss at the hollow just below her throat, then dragged her body against his while he opened her door and urged her inside. "I should like to go home now, my Elise. If you find that idea agreeable."

She blinked as if coming out of a trance. "Yes. Let's go home. Right now."

Each night, Caspian stared at the sky, mentally keeping track of how the moon shifted, growing rounder and fuller with each new darkness. Pressure built behind his eyes. He was due home in Atlantis soon. If he didn't return on the designated tide, he feared his father would send someone to retrieve him.

He could not forget that although very few Mer had the capability to visit land, there did exist some. His father for one, and his cousin Maui. And rumors circulated of another—younger than him by perhaps 300 tides—already being groomed as a future guardian of the gate. Caspian had been away for many, many tides. Perhaps his father had found others by now.

He'd avoided swimming in the sea at all costs, but after so many weeks, the potency of his poison-soaked necklace grew weak. Soon, he would be forced to return to the privacy of his cove in order to swim—this would renew his lungs and expel infection from his gills—it would eventually become a requirement of his survival ashore.

And still, Elise did not know.

Chapter Eleven

PLAGUED BY FATIGUE, ELISE STRUGGLED to finish her shift. Halfway through, her stomach bubbled dangerously, and her head ached so badly that she wondered if she was fighting off a cold. Since Caspian had begun sharing her bed, she wasn't getting her normal amount of sleep—being occupied with his nearness and the heat of his skin so close to hers, whether touching or not. She pushed through another hour, until weak, shaking arms left her at risk of dumping the loaded tray all over a customer, and finally called in Maggie to cover the rest of her shift.

Caspian still had a couple of hours to finish at his new job, and when she called the resort, he insisted that he could get back on his own, so for the first time in ages, Elise went home alone.

She woke from her nap as the last of the sun's rays dipped beneath the horizon, the sky already fading from blue, to gray, as it inched toward inky night. She tossed back her blankets, yawning, and crawled out of bed, still fighting nausea, but also starving. She hoped that Caspian had thought to concoct some sort of food, since he'd begun to experiment in the kitchen from time to time.

A chill had crept into the house, warning of an oncoming storm, so she pulled a throw blanket around her shoulders and stumbled into the living room, confused about the unusual silence. She'd grown accustomed to having another person around, and found the noises of companionship comforting. "Caspian?" She flipped on the light, noticing that her shoes waited on the floor, just out of the walkway where she'd left them, and her purse on the table near the door. She'd stripped herself of both as she'd come inside, bypassing everything else to crawl straight into her bed. This illness, whatever it was, had taken a toll, and she'd hoped Caspian would step up and help care for her, the way she'd cared for him when they'd first met.

He'd adjusted well to life in Oceanside. So well that she often forgot that he wasn't native to the city, or the country, for that matter. The difference in customs had proven different during their first week together, but he'd picked up on social traditions quickly, so well that even his speech patterns had begun to change. Sometimes he almost sounded like an American.

When she flipped on the kitchen light and found the space exactly as it had been when they'd left that morning, a shiver of panic sent her brain spiraling. He should have been off work almost two hours ago. What if he was stranded at the resort? Or if he'd gotten lost on his way home? What if he'd accepted a ride from a serial killer?

Stomach churning, and still wrapped in the blanket, she snatched her keys and drew on the nearest pair of flip-flops, darting to the car to launch a search for the man she'd once found wandering aimlessly in a cemetery. What if Marcus had been right in thinking that Caspian had serious mental issues. What if he'd snapped again?

Her hands shook as she pulled into the resort parking lot and parked the car. She'd never visited this place before meeting Caspian, but now considered it a special place for them—one she hoped wouldn't be tainted by the memory of some horrible accident or other disaster that had kept Caspian from getting home on time. She pushed through the gate, bypassing a gift shop, a snack stand, and a beach rental booth as she headed for the children's pool. Only a smattering of children remained, most supervised by parents. The two on-duty lifeguards waved, but she recognized neither. She had only met one of Caspian's new friends. He had come into The Sea Turtle specifically to introduce himself to her.

That friend, Peter, rounded the path between the kiddie pool and the adult one, his steps slowing when he saw Elise, still wrapped in her blanket, on the verge of tears. "Have you seen Caspian?" Her voice shook, giving away her surging fear.

Peter checked his watch, frowning. "Not for a couple of hours. He left just after four. Something wrong? Do you need help?"

Elise swallowed a lump in her throat, making a conscious effort to not grind her teeth. "I just . . . I haven't seen him. I left work early because I wasn't feeling well, and he should have been home by now."

Peter pursed his lips, folding his arms across his scrawny chest. "Maybe he had errands to run. Or stopped to visit friends."

She shook her head, denial burning in her veins. "No. He's not from here. He doesn't know anyone except me. And now you." It was possible he'd finally found his mother, but she couldn't believe that he would up and leave her without at least saying goodbye.

Peter hollered at the lifeguard watching over the water slide. "Have you seen Cas?"

The lifeguard pointed down the beach, shouting something Elise couldn't quite hear.

Peter patted Elise's shoulder and steered her toward the exit gate. "You know Caspian. He loves his walks on the sand." He glanced at his watch, then at the sky as if gauging the exact shade of indigo. "I wouldn't worry too much. Probably be back any time, now."

She did worry. Since she'd met him, Elise had suspected that Caspian kept multiple secrets. Important ones. And then there was the abandoned search for his long-lost mother. Until now, Elise hadn't wanted to pry, and had instead been living in denial that her lover would, at some point, feel the urge to pick up where he'd left off, and eventually go home to— wherever he was from. But she hoped they would have more time together. What would happen when he finally found what he'd come here looking for?

She jogged down the beach until her breath came in short, harsh spurts and her knees ached from the impact of her feet on the sand. Until the blanket flew behind her like a cape and the chilly air curled around her, numbing her nose, cheeks, fingers, and toes—and still there was no sign of him. Miles from the resort, she stopped, gasping for breath, chest heaving with ache. Could he truly have left her without a word?

Desperate to rest, she planted herself in the sand, tightening the blanket around her and tucking her face into her knees while hot tears filled her eyes. Why had she left him behind? Why was she such a wimp that she'd had to go home early? She'd never done that— not since her father died.

More time passed, and the inky sky brightened as the moon climbed, almost full, reflecting an eerie sapphire glow off the surface of the water each time it peeked out from behind the darkening clouds. Eventually, cold seeped through her blanket and soaked into her, and Elise stood, knowing she needed to go home, take care of herself, but still unable to leave without Caspian.

A distant voice yelled, "Elise?"

She squinted through the darkness, eyes straining to outline the figure jogging toward her. "Caspian?" It only took seconds of watching him move, so rigidly upright, with shoulders squared and muscles bulging, to identify her love. She bolted to him, hurling herself into his arms with a sob. "I thought you'd left me. I thought . . . so many horrible things. Where have you been? Why didn't you come home after work, like you promised?"

He held her against him, pressing a kiss to the top of her head. "I am sorry you worried. I would never leave you in such a way. I could not."

Dampness seeped through his clothes, and water dripped from his hair, along his shoulders and down his back, sliding over Elise's skin. "Did you go swimming again?"

He hesitated, which caused jealous suspicion to rear inside her. "I did, yes."

She jerked away, emotions at war as she tightened her blanket, colder than ever, now that her T-shirt was damp. "It's freezing out. You're going to get sick. Why would you go swimming in the ocean, when you've spent all day working at a pool?"

He draped a protective arm around her, leading her back toward the parking lot. "Salt water is more cleansing than chemically treated pool-water. I am used to cooler temperatures."

A wave of dizziness hit, so she tipped her head and leaned on his shoulder. "It's freezing. I'm freezing."

Caspian stopped, as if suddenly realizing that she wasn't okay. He pressed a hand to her forehead, her cheek, then slid one arm behind her back, and the other beneath her knees, sweeping her into his arms. "You're unwell, my beloved. Let us go home."

She held tight to his neck as her head drooped against his chest. "Yes, please. I need a hot bath. And soup. And snuggles." She burrowed into him, shivers wracking her again.

"And you shall have it all, my love. I will make sure of it."

He followed through on his promise, starting with drawing her a hot bath, and then—with specific instructions—managed to heat up a can of noodle soup. Both soothed Elise tremendously, and she told him as much. But every time he left the room, insecure emotions flooded her again. He hadn't left her today, but he would eventually.

She'd allowed him his secrets, without demanding answers, because he held onto them so tight, and she already consumed so much of him, but now her instincts asserted that those secrets weren't small. The longer he stayed, the more important it was for her to know the truth. All of it.

The ache she experienced during those long, miserable hours—when she believed that he'd left without a goodbye—had been an eye-opening experience. Though Caspian was now only one room away in the tiny, cottage-style house, a gulf had opened between them, and her side had already begun to fill with grief. Up to this point, losing her father had been the most grief she'd ever believed a person could feel, but now she worried that losing Caspian would be even more excruciating, especially since he would leave by choice. She prayed that when it happened, she would find some way to survive.

Once she was dry and settled into bed, Caspian slid in too, shifting her into his arms and demanding nothing, but to hold her while she slept. It was the most sweetly intimate night they'd ever spent together.

Chapter Twelve

THE NEED TO SWIM HIT him in the way of a rip-tide, sucking the air from his lungs and squeezing tight in his chest, head, and throat, until Caspian was forced to leave work an hour early. Knowing Elise would come looking for him, he asked Peter to call The Sea Turtle so he could speak with her—warn her that he would find his way home when he was able.

She picked up the phone, sounding surprised to have received a call. "Yes?"

Caspian turned away from Peter, taking three big steps from the concrete to the sand. "Hello my beloved. Please do not worry if I am not here when you finish your work. There is something I must do, but I will return soon after you arrive."

Dishes clinked on her end, and a low hum of voices filled the void. After several long seconds, Elise cleared her throat and croaked, "What do you have to do? Where are you going?"

"It is nothing to worry about." He picked a half-smashed hibiscus flower off the ground, twirling it between his fingers. "I promise that I will be home soon."

Her breath caught. "Why can't you tell me? You know everything about me, and I know so little about you, and I just . . . I don't like this feeling. It's confusing and it hurts."

The pain, evident in her voice, reminded him how important it was for him to tell her everything, the way he'd been planning, and had continued to put off—but he couldn't do it over the phone, and as his chest squeezed tighter, he knew he couldn't wait until she finished her work. He closed the bud gently in his fist, careful to protect the un-smashed petals from further damage. "I will tell you everything tonight, once I reach home." He recalled an earlier conversation, during which Peter and the lifeguards discussed their favorite takeout restaurants. "Peter has told me about a marvelous place where I can order food that is already prepared, and bring it home for eating. I received money from my job today, so I will do this thing on my way home, and provide our nightly meal, as you have done so often for me."

"Lots of places do take out, Caspian. We do that here, at the Turtle. Which one did Peter tell you about that you're so anxious to try?"

He glanced at Peter, shrugging as he tried to remember the name of the place, and finally answered with, "It is a stand where the cooks prepare seafood on the beach, including crab, which is my favorite."

Elise sighed, and it sounded more shaky than usual. This worried Caspian, so he decided he should pick her some flowers on the way home. He would have to make peace for not sharing his secrets sooner. "Fine. Just don't get anything that smells too fishy. My stomach is still tender."

Caspian ended the call, and returned the phone to Peter. "Thank you for the use of your communication device. I must leave now." He clocked out, running down the beach toward the cove, his desperation to swim clawing at his throat in wheezes and thick swelling. When he arrived—a distance humans would measure in miles—he crept around and across a narrow strip of land between cliffs, and shimmied his way into the cave, realizing as he got there that he'd held onto the flower all this way. He opened his fist, hoping he'd managed to save it, only to realize that he'd crushed the thing into his skin, leaving almost no trace of the soft, silky petals that he had originally picked up.

This, he decided, did not bode well for him.

He brushed the petals from his hands, and, having wised up after the last time Elise had almost caught him swimming, stripped off his clothes and left them in a heap on the sand before diving into the shallow inlet that would expel him to the open sea.

Though he had no human timepiece, he did his best to keep his time as short as possible, avoiding any expanses where predators were known to lurk. If the inlet had been slightly deeper, he would have remained near the cove, protected from the prying eyes of the merman who was assigned to guard the entrance to the Atlantian gate, and the attention of whom he hoped to avoid.

As he glided around a barnacle-covered cannon, he concocted a magnificent idea to gather underwater treasures, which he could fashion into a gift for Elise. Perhaps such a thing would soften her anger and help her to understand that while he had no desire to return to Atlantis yet, his survival commanded that he swim at regular intervals—whether he wanted to or not.

He headed for an area where deep water oysters were known to nest, but as his pendant banged against his chest, he realized that pearls were not of much value in this case—at least, not valuable enough for his precious Elise. He changed course and veered, instead, to a shipwreck that his father's explorers had discovered only tides before Caspian departed for his adventures on land. This portion of a ship had carried sparkling stones of many colors, as well as a shimmery substance not unlike the adornment that Elise sometimes wore around her neck.

Though his father had designated an entire cave to storing the treasures his people harvested from human wreckage, Caspian felt confident that what remained at the site would not be missed—by his father or the explorers. He filled a tin vessel—which he now recognized as a bowl—with a variety of the items, and hurried back to the cove, careful not to spill his wares and leave a trail for the Mer to discover.

Triumphant with his find, Caspian glided into the inlet, and set the bowl on the edge, and then dragged himself out of the water, where he stood naked, his scales having not yet receded into his skin. A pained gasp snapped his attention to the back of the cave, where Elise sat, holding his clothes on her lap, tears trailing down her cheeks as if she'd been sitting there for quite some time.

"Elise," he murmured, wondering how she'd found him, why she'd come here instead of returning home as he'd requested. "I wanted to tell you . . ."

"What?" she shouted? "What did you want to tell me? Who is out there with you?"

He whirled around, now worried that Marietta or the guard had followed him. When he didn't see any traces of others, he returned his focus to Elise. "There is no one here but you and me. I have brought you a surprise."

She squeezed his clothes into her chest as more tears fell. "I don't want a present from you right now. I want answers. All of them."

"I will provide them to you. What are your questions?"

She shook her head, vigorously objecting. "Nope. No hints. Just tell me everything. Start from the beginning. Like, why would you come all this way—on foot—to swim, when we both work right on a beach? Why aren't you wearing any clothes? And how did you stay underwater for such a long time without coming up for air?"

Since she held his clothes hostage, he approached and sat next to her in the sand. He tried to take her hand, but she pulled it back, refusing his touch for the first time since they'd met. Finally, he confessed, "I am from a faraway place, called Atlantis. This city is located beneath the sea, where I live with the Mer, because I am one. Or, half one. I am also half human, due to my mother's heritage, which is partly how I am able to come ashore and breathe on land."

She shook her head in denial, then tossed his clothes in his lap as if suddenly realizing that he was still naked. "There are no such things as mermaids."

Again, he tried to take her hand, but she still refused. "There is. We exist." He drew her attention to the scars on his neck—scars that had not yet closed completely. "Gills." He tapped his pendant. "Not long ago, I met my cousin Maui, who possessed a substance—a strong poison—that, when infused into soft stones such as pearls, like these—paralyzes our gills, forcing those of us who were born with lungs to fill those lungs with oxygen, and learn to breathe ashore. Each time the effect of the poison weakens, my body requires that I swim in the salt water to clear out my gills, which act as a filter for my newly-activated lungs."

"You can't possibly expect me to believe this." Elise's teeth chattered from the way her body shook. Caspian couldn't tell if anxiety or anger or perhaps even shock, made her tremble so, but each time he attempted to wrap a protective arm around her, to pull her against him for support, she shrugged it away and put more distance between them, so he let her be.

"It is truth." Experiencing a wave of his own anxiety, Caspian stood and dragged on his shorts, and then his T-shirt, before sitting next to Elise again. "This is why my speech differs from yours, and why so much of your culture is foreign to me. I lived in this city as a youngling, but do not remember much of my mother— only that my father snatched me away from her on this very beach—" he pointed in the direction from which they'd come. "And he brought me to Atlantis, where I am Prince, someday to be King, and where everything

114

in my life has been according to my father's will, including the mermaid to whom I was betrothed, only tides after my arrival in Atlantis."

A tear rolled down Elise's cheek, and Caspian ached to hold her. "I'm having a really hard time comprehending this. All of it. But I do understand the part about you being engaged." She shook her head, refusing his touch again, and Caspian's shoulders drooped in misery. "I know that you're not staying in Oceanside permanently. I've always known you'll have to leave someday, but this . . . all of it, is a massive reminder to me that staying or leaving truly isn't your choice. It hurts. I don't want it to, and I know you don't mean for it to, but it still hurts."

"My love, this is not easy for me either—" he started, but Elise stood, pacing the small space with furious, heavy steps.

"You aren't the one who'll be left behind to pick up the pieces," she sobbed. "When you leave here, you'll be going home to family, and to a woman who, like her or not, is your intended. And, apparently, to a job as royalty. That's got to be a million times better than lifeguarding at the resort. I understand why you'd want those things. Who wouldn't? But when you go back to your life, I'm left here alone, all over again. No family, no boyfriend, and still working my ridiculous job at The Turtle just to keep food in my kitchen."

Caspian stood, returning to the water's edge to retrieve the bowl he'd brought from the shipwreck. "Elise, I do not wish to leave you. You are my beloved, and the only female who matters in my life—aside from perhaps my mother, for whom I have not searched in weeks. I wish to not leave you in pieces." He offered her the bowl. "I do not know the value of these treasures, but it is much in the human world. I collected them for your benefit, so that when I am forced to leave, you will still be able to rest on days when you are unwell."

Her eyes widened as her fingers trailed over the gemstones and gold. "You're right. These are worth a lot." But moments later, anger darkened her eyes and she knocked the bowl from his hand, sending the contents spilling to the ground. "I don't want your money, Caspian. Or your jewels. Don't you understand? I've fallen in love with you. I know that was a stupid thing to do, but it happened, nonetheless. Do you think that paying me off will make me feel better about knowing you're leaving?" She balled up her fist and took a swing at him, but he grabbed her shoulders and pulled her into his chest, keeping her safe, unable to hurt herself in her fury.

"Elise," he croaked, finding his throat felt full of fluid. "You are my beloved, now and forever. The Mer do not join for love—it is not an emotion many are familiar with, as few are allowed such luxuries. But I have known it with you, and I cannot let it go. I will never let it go."

She pressed her face into his chest, cheeks wet from tears. "But you're going to let *me* go, aren't you?"

Was he? In this moment, as in so many that had come before, holding Elise left him questioning everything about his life and future. The idea of leaving her behind when he returned to Atlantis caused his insides to rumble with a curious pain that simply could not be removed. Still, he had obligations, a successional order that depended upon his return and the production of an heir. Until he could offer his father another solution, he could not make promises to Elise, for he would not be able to keep them. "I do not want to." he assured her. But still didn't offer to try and stay.

Elise cried into his chest, her fist clutching his T-shirt and dragging at it to wipe her eyes. When she had composed herself, she left the circle of his arms, her expression blank as she sniffled. "Are you coming home tonight? I need to go. I can't stay here anymore."

Caspian glanced at the treasures spilled over the ground. "I am coming now. With you, if you will allow."

She swallowed, nodded, then bent to pick up a sharply pointed green stone. "This might be an emerald. Emeralds are my favorite."

Following her lead, Caspian bent to gather the stones and replace them in the bowl, which he brought with them as they made their way around the narrow strip of land near the cliffs. When they arrived at the path that had originally led him to the cemetery where they'd met, he thought to explain to her that part of his story. But while he stopped, Elise continued on, unwilling to wait on him any longer, so he left the story for later and followed her down the beach to get her car.

That night, at her request, Caspian returned to sleep in Elise's father's bed, leaving the chasm between them to grow wider.

Chapter Thirteen

BETWEEN TEARS AND HER QUEASY stomach, Elise didn't sleep much. She lay awake for most of the night, listening to the wind howl and the clouds boom with thunder, and by the wee hours of morning, rain pattering against her window. The logical side of her brain reminded her that she had known Caspian had secrets, that he was only here temporarily. But logic couldn't compose the emotions raging through every pour, every blood vessel, every nerve in her body.

Practical-Elise knew that Caspian hadn't forced her to fall in love with him, that he wasn't choosing to leave her, and that he was trapped by an obligation to his own family—something she understood well. But emotional-Elise couldn't separate grief, from anger, from blame.

She experienced such a range of feelings that by morning, her brain had exhausted itself, even as her body refused to allow her to sleep.

Breakfast became a solemn affair. She met Caspian in the kitchen and brewed coffee in silence, while he made the one breakfast food he'd figured out—toast. They sat in awkward silence, across the table from one another, but a million miles apart. When she dropped him at the resort for his shift, the only thing left in her was relief.

At work, she got two orders wrong and dropped an entire plate of gooey eggs on the floor of the dining room. When she forgot to give Marcus the order from a table, and the customers waited almost an hour with no food, Marcus called her into the kitchen for a chat.

"You're off today. What's wrong?"

How could she explain all the things going through her head? She couldn't exactly tell people that her boyfriend was a merman from the lost city of Atlantis. She was still struggling to comprehend it herself. If they believed that explanation, Caspian would become a science experiment, while hundreds of treasure-seekers launched searches for the illusive hidden city. If they didn't believe her story—well, Marcus was likely to think Elise had lost her mind, far more than he ever thought was the case with Caspian, and she'd end up at the mental hospital where she'd once promised to take him.

"Just tired. I didn't sleep well last night."

Marcus mixed pancake batter for their weekend brunch and poured six round dollops on the griddle. "You still not feeling well, or is trouble brewing between you and the crazy man?"

Too exhausted for jokes, Elise leaned on the wall, not even cracking a smile. "Both. I think I just need a break."

Marcus paused, spatula in hand, and focused on Elise. "He hasn't hurt you, has he?"

"No. He wouldn't." She shook her head, unwilling to sic Marcus on poor Caspian, who was clearly as distraught as Elise. She didn't know what to do about any of it, but getting Marcus involved was definitely not an answer.

"Glad to hear that." Marcus returned to his pancakes, an embarrassed blush creeping into his cheeks. "Are you pregnant?"

The very suggestion had Elise straightening in defense. "Of course not. I'm not that stupid. I . . . we . . . ." The truth was, she hadn't given much thought to birth control. She'd taken the pill in high school, at her father's insistence, but had never had a true need, and after an infection that sent her to the ER last winter, her doctor had suggested she go off them for a while. And she'd taken his advice. Caspian obviously didn't know a *thing* about birth control. Which brought up the question of whether or not he could even produce human children? He hadn't seemed concerned about the risks, so Elise had to assume it wasn't a worry. "I just need a nap. I think I'm still fighting that cold from last week. Do you mind if I leave for a while? I promise to come back in time for the afternoon rush."

Marcus waved her away. "Might as well. Not doing me much good here, dropping entrees and forgetting orders. I'll let you go on the condition that you promise to see a doctor sometime in the next few days— make sure you don't have something worse than a cold. I worry about you."

She worried about her too. Elise shoved her hand in her apron pocket to withdraw the phone list she kept there. "Do you want me to call Shelley to cover?"

Marcus checked the pass-through window, and seemed satisfied with Maggie's abilities. "We can survive until you come back. Just don't take more than two hours."

She retreated to the locker area, phone list still in hand as she untied her apron. When she realized that she hadn't replaced the page, she went to shove it back in the pocket, surprised to find that it wasn't actually the phone list—but the message that woman had left for Caspian, long before he'd gotten his job. She crinkled the paper in her hand, tears welling all over again. She couldn't keep this from him any longer— but what would happen when she told him?

Unable to think with any sort of logic, she shoved the paper in her purse and slammed her locker shut, determined to sleep first—think later.

Because of her extended break, Caspian got off work before Elise, and since he'd gone swimming the day before—and claimed he was now okay to wait a few days—he came to the Turtle to await the end of her shift. The dinner rush had packed the place, leaving no empty tables where he could sit, and Elise knew that Marcus wasn't comfortable having Caspian hang out in the break room. Though the rain had passed, an early fall chill had settled in the air. It would soon dissolve, leaving the remaining summer days to scorch the last of the vegetation, but in the meantime, Elise refused to send Caspian outside to wait in the cold.

She intended to send him after the takeout he'd promised the day before. A sort-of peace offering. She still didn't have answers, but after some sleep, her mind was clearer, and she'd awoken aching with loss. If their time together was limited, they couldn't afford to waste another night sleeping in separate rooms.

When he arrived, she met him at the back door with a kiss and a smile. "Hey. Last night you promised me seafood takeout, and we never got it. How do you feel about paying up? You could go get our order while I finish my shift, and we could take it home after."

Caspian closed in, caution in his every move until Elise slid her arms around his middle, at which point he embraced her as well. "I would like that very much. I am sorry to have hurt you."

Elise closed her eyes and shook her head, not wanting to start the fight over again while her emotions still hung on edge. "Do you have money or should I get you some?"

He withdrew a folded check from his pocket and handed it to her. "I have this. I am told it is worth many green bills."

Elise giggled as a crash sounded from the dining room. "You're so cute. Yes, it's worth many bills, but you have to take it to a bank to get those bills. You can't spend it like this. No one will accept it."

He frowned at the check as Marcus called for Elise. Torn, Elise punched in the combination for her locker then stalked to find out what had been broken. "Just get my wallet out of my locker. There should be some cash in there. We can cash your check tomorrow." With a sassy swat on Caspian's bottom, she winked, and then sauntered through the dining-room door to help close the place up.

An hour later, Elise had pushed the last customers out the door and wiped down all the tables. She untied her apron on her way to the back, relieved to remove the tight ribbon that held it in place. She hooked it on the knob belonging to her, then went to remove her handbag from the locker, only to find it gone.

A cough from the chair in the corner had her whipping around. Caspian sat as still as stone in the single recliner, eyes glaring with the hurt of a thousand molten pokers stabbing him.

"What?" she asked, hurrying to him. "What's wrong? What's happened?"

He opened his fist and offered her the crumpled page on which the woman had written her contact information. "I found this in your bag when I went looking for money. I still do not read well, but I remember more each day. These are a combination of numbers used for calling someone on the phone. They belong to a woman who came in search of me."

Her mouth worked, but no sound came out as she leaned on the wall for support. "I was going to tell you about that, it's just that I got sick, and then I sort of forgot until earlier today. I had planned to tell you tonight, see what you want to do next."

The glare didn't leave her face, and he barely blinked. "Elise, you know I've come here to find my mother. This is very important, not only to me, but to all the Mer of Atlantis. How long have you had this in your possession?"

The question had her squirming. She didn't want to lie to Caspian—even after he'd all-but lied to her—but neither did she have the courage to give him the full truth. She'd had it since the week when they'd first made love, and had kept it from him all this time. "A while."

He leaned forward in the chair, elbows to knees, refusing to take his eyes off her face. "Finding my mother could change everything. This is important information. I cannot believe you have kept this from me."

"It . . . it wasn't on purpose," she insisted, pressing her back against the lockers. "I was going to tell you."

"As I was going to tell you about my history, my heritage. And now we both know that we have kept secrets from one another. I do not know what to do next, but I did not purchase our take-out-food, so perhaps Turtle burgers will be tonight's meal."

Elise nodded, stunned mute. He'd become so cold compared to when she'd seen him only an hour ago. "I'm sorry, Caspian. I never intended to let you down or to ignore the information I know you need so desperately. I would never intentionally keep you from your mother." Even though a part of her wished she could keep him all to herself, for always.

126

"I have used the phone here to dial this number, and the female on the other end has the same voice I remember. She will be meeting me in this parking lot at nine a.m. tomorrow. If she is truly my mother, you will have kept her from me all this time. I do not believe you would have told me tonight, as you claim."

"I would have. I meant to, I just—" Elise swallowed, feeling like a black hole had opened in the floor and waited to swallow her. "If she *is* your mother, does that mean you're leaving?"

Caspian stood, pushing past her on his way out the door. "I do not know where we go from here, but I can no longer delay the objective of my visit. I must call on my mother."

Chapter Fourteen

THEY RODE HOME IN TENSE silence, both lost in the misery of their thoughts. Caspian scrutinized Elise. Why she would keep such important information hidden? Why hadn't she told him immediately? Shared the happy news that would allow him to fill in that gaps felt in his life and heart?

Her eyes glistened with unshed tears, and when one fell, she silently wiped it away, refusing to acknowledge that it had fallen at all. When he'd told her that love was not something the Mer understood well, it was sheer, painful truth. His father had chosen Caspian's mate-to-be, and such arrangements were customary among the Mer. Joining with a mate ensured survival of the species, and caused the city to flourish with growth and prosperity. His own father had shown very little love to the child who had been stolen from his mother, the merboy who cried oceans over the loss of his true family, and who had eventually adjusted to his new life out of necessity, rather than desire.

Love brought him across the blue sea to spend time upon the dry, brown shore in search of that person he'd lost—and not just the person, the feeling. Love. Once a distant memory, now a flood of confusion and emotion so overwhelming as to leave his brain bobbing between dangerous, uncharted territories.

He hadn't meant to drag Elise into it, had never intended to love her the way he did, but he had also been too naïve to know how to avoid such things. He had never understood that this feeling could be shared with a mate, that the happiness he experienced with her would cause him to question everything about his life, and his plans for the future. He did not know what should, or would come next, but the distance between him and his beloved grew with each passing moment. Whatever happened now, their time together had likely come to the end—and that thought stole his breath in a way that felt completely different from needing to purge his gills.

What if this was their last night together?

They arrived home having not exchanged a single word between them, but once the door closed out the night, he could no longer take the silence. "Elise, I do not wish to fight. I am angry, and you are angry, and we do not know what tomorrow brings. Perhaps I shall finally meet my mother. Perhaps not. Soon I must return to my home and report to Father—it is my duty. I do not wish to spend my remaining nights ashore sleeping apart from you."

Two tears broke free and trailed down her cheeks, and she wiped them away with her fingertips. "I don't either."

He approached her with a new degree of shyness, a deeper level of need, opening his arms to bring her back into the space between them—the space that belonged only to her—and when she clung to him, sniffling, deep wells of emotion battled wars inside him. If he were to join with Marietta, or any other mermaid, he could never feel for them—or anyone— the way he felt for Elise. The devastating realization hit him as a blow to the gut. No matter what choice he made, or what possibilities remained, he would lose something enormously important to him. He was not sure how to survive either loss.

He resisted his imminent defeat, by pressing his lips to Elise's, drawing her toward the bedroom where they'd spent so much time together in recent weeks. He no longer needed food, or explanations or words of sorrow. He would not make a promise that he could not keep. But this—he could give her this, as she could give to him. If this night was all they could take and keep of each other, he vowed to make it worth the suffering that was sure to follow.

"Do you want me to wait out here with you?" Elise stood next to Caspian in the parking lot, holding his hand, touching his arm, brushing back his hair as if she were more nervous than him. He did not understand why, and having her present as he waited for his mother felt wrong, somehow, as if the two lines could not be crossed.

He directed her back to the car. "No. I must do this alone. I am sorry."

Her chin quivered, eyelashes fluttering, but she clenched her jaw and replied with a curt nod. "Okay. I'm going to . . ." She glanced at the car, the street, the restaurant. "I'm going inside to talk to Marcus. That way, if something goes wrong, I won't have to come back to pick you up. Or even if it doesn't go wrong, I just . . . I'll be nearby."

Caspian shored up his courage, taking a deep breath and squaring his shoulders. "I will be fine. Nothing will go wrong."

Elise slung her purse over her shoulder and twirled her keys around her finger, swallowing hard. "If you're right, if this *is* her, will I . . . I mean, should I expect to hear from you again? Tonight, or tomorrow or . . . sometime?"

A car rolled past, stealing his attention. When it didn't turn into the lot, his eyes remained fixed on the road, waiting, while his stomach knotted and unknotted in quick, rapid actions. "I do not know."

"Can you at least try?" Her voice cracked. "Maybe just once before you go home to Atlantis?"

His attention flicked to her, then back to the street, unable to focus on Elise while his mind spun with all the questions that had built up over the years. "I shall try, yes. But please do not be angry with me if I cannot."

What if his mother did not have a phone? What if she did not want him to stay near? What if his mother was angry that he'd left and stayed gone for so long? What if she did not wish him to see Elise again?

Or what if she had another family? A new one, with a new son?

Elise sniffled behind him. "Can you at least look at me while I'm trying to say goodbye?"

He turned, eyes on Elise, but his mind still drowning in questions. "Goodbye, my beloved. I will never forget our time together."

Tears rolled down her cheeks, and this time she didn't wipe them away. She threw her arms around him, squeezing harder than she ever had. "I'll never forget you either. Ever. Please try to at least let me know you're okay. Whenever you can."

He hugged her back, then set her away from him, urging her to leave. "It is almost time. I must prepare myself for this important moment."

Sniffling again, Elise nodded, then turned away and ran inside.

Minutes later, a beat up blue car turned into the lot—a car Caspian recognized from his childhood. The car stopped in the middle of the row, just short of hitting him, and a woman got out. She wasn't tall, perhaps five-foot four, with dark hair and sharp cheek bones and a slender build that reminded Caspian how young his mother had been when he was born. From what he could tell, she didn't have a single skin wrinkle, as many older humans did. After having seen himself in Elise's mirror every morning for the last few weeks, he recognized many features present in her face that he'd also noticed in his own.

"Caspian," she said, opening her arms with a grin.

He ran to her, picking her up as he accepted her embrace. "Mother."

"Welcome home, my son."

Chapter Fifteen

THE DAYS PASSED LIKE A blur of time. Each night, Elise slept in the bed she'd shared with Caspian. His scent lingered on the sheets, on his pillow, the memories of all they'd shared, causing a physical ache in her chest, heaviness that refused to lift. When morning came, she forced herself out of bed, forced herself to shower and dress, forced coffee down her throat, and attempted to nibble on toast—but she couldn't force herself to eat much more, no matter what time of day.

She painted on a false smile and did her job as best as she could manage, gathered her tips, and then returned home. She no longer laughed with Marcus and the other waitresses, or flirted with the customers. And she refused to even so much as look at the beach, let alone walk on it.

After two weeks of numb despondency, Marcus paid her a visit at home in the middle of the day. He knocked first, and then walked in as if he owned the place—something he'd never done when her father was alive, and it said a lot about his degree of concern. "Elise? Are you here?"

"Yes, I'm here." She'd spent most of the night in the bathroom, dry-heaving from what must have been either moldy bread, or a virus, and emerged with her hair a tangled, matted mess, still wearing her father's flannel pajamas—the ones she'd loaned to Caspian—and wrapped in the comforter from her bed.

Marcus stood inside the door, taking in the disastrous state of her home, the garbage that had piled up to the lid of the can, stacks of dishes on the coffee table and in the sink, a carton of eggs left out on the counter—she couldn't even remember having taken them out of the fridge—and piles of tissues strung throughout it all. "You're not okay, are you?"

She blinked, rapidly, as emotion rose to her sinuses and leaked out all over again. It was embarrassing that she couldn't stop crying, even when she was alone. "I'm fine. I'll be fine."

Marcus moved in and wrapped an awkward arm around her shoulders. "No, you're not. You're depressed, and it shows."

"I'm not depressed." She pulled away, dragging her comforter behind her while she sat on the sofa. Her muscles ached from standing. Comfort had become a luxury that only existed in her memory. Marcus followed, choosing to sit in the adjacent recliner. "I'm hurt, but I'm getting over it. I'm lonely, but I'll learn to live with it—always have. And I'm sick. Can't seem to kick this virus. I think I've overworked my body lately, and it's taking revenge."

Marcus pressed his palms against the arms of the chair. "Did you ever see a doctor, like you promised?"

She picked up a tissue and wiped her eyes and nose. "Can't afford it. I can barely afford food these days." Not that she needed food. In the deep, dark recesses of her mind, starving to death sounded like a mercy.

"I'll pay for it," Marcus insisted. "It's time for you to get checked out. I'm worried about you. And not just your mental health—though I worry about that, too." From the way his attention darted around, Elise gathered that he didn't approve of her current living conditions.

"Thank you, Marcus, but I can't accept that." She twisted the tissue in her hand, wrapping it between fingers, and then smoothing it out flat again.

"You can, and you will. I'm not insisting on this as your friend, but as your employer. I can't have my best waitress falling apart at work and being too sick to do the job. And I know you need the money, so I can't make you stay home when you're having days like . . ."

he made a point of openly evaluating her current condition. "Today."

She tugged at her unwashed pajamas, uncomfortable with Marcus's assessment. "I don't work for two more hours. As I always do, I'll show up clean and presentable, and I'll do my best not to infect the customers. I haven't let you down yet, not the whole time I've worked for you."

"No, you haven't." He sat back and folded his arms across his chest. "But it concerns me that you're still in bed at one o'clock in the afternoon on a sunny, late-summer day. I've never known you to be a hermit, even after your father died."

"Why shouldn't I sleep in, if I want to? I'm an adult, and I didn't sleep well last night because of the wind, and other noises. Besides, I don't want to go outside. It's too bright, and too hot, and . . . and . . ."

"And Caspian might be out there."

She shook her head, refusing to acknowledge that fear, though it was real. She wasn't sure how she'd react, or how she'd feel if she were to run into him on the beach and he ignored her, or treated her the way he had in the parking lot that last day.

"Look." Marcus stood, removing two business cards from his pocket and dropping them on Elise's lap. "You're going to call both of those numbers today, before you go to work, and make appointments. Two of them. One at the clinic, and one with a therapist. I'm paying for both, so you have no excuses."

She stood, letting the cards tumble to the ground. "You're not my father, Marcus. You can't *make* me get medical treatment."

He bent to pick up the cards, and then held them in front of her face, eyes narrowed in anger. "I'm the closest thing you've got, and I, your boss, have the right to require doctor visits when there is reason to be concerned. Look it up in the state law book. You do this, Elise, or I'll cut your hours back until you get well again."

Anger pressed against the sadness, funneling into a swirl of emotions that almost, almost reached her mouth in the form of words—but the eddy died before those words could form, and all the anger, sadness, emotion of any kind, fizzled into nothing. Less than nothing. Maybe she was less okay than she thought. "I can't afford to have my hours cut, Marcus. And you're already short on waitresses. Cutting my hours would only hurt us both."

"I know." He pressed the cards into her hand and dropped a kiss on her forehead. "That's why I know you'll make these calls and get whatever treatment you need. You're too dependable to do anything else."

She snorted, tucking the blanket more tightly around her. "Dependable. Now that's a trait to keep.

Winning hearts all over the world, with that one, clearly."

Marcus gripped her shoulders in support. "He hurt you. We all know it. These things happen, Elise. Sometimes relationships end badly, and it sucks. It's okay to grieve, to admit that you're suffering. But it's not okay to let a broken heart dump you into a hole and leave you there. You're stronger than that."

Hearing this perspective from Marcus, of all people, hit her directly in the place where her most tender feelings lingered, so she threw her arms around him and took a thing she hadn't realized she badly needed. A hug.

A month passed, and when she hadn't heard from Caspian, Elise resigned herself to the knowledge that he was gone.

The therapist Marcus referred her to had a long wait list, and so did the doctor. She opted to go without the first, but made an appointment with the second, though the first available opening was weeks away. Having Marcus in her living room had reminded Elise of the last time he'd visited, just after her father died. How she'd struggled, and sobbed, and withdrawn, and then accepted the loss and chosen to move forward. How strong she'd been back then. She could find that strength again now, she decided, and began taking steps to rid herself of the ache that held her immobile.

First, she cleaned her house, top to bottom, until it sparkled—kitchen, bathroom, closets and cabinets. Second, she decided it was time to clear out her father's room and move into it herself. She owned the house, now, after all. There was no reason she should continue living in the smaller of the two bedrooms, allowing grime to accumulate in the luxurious master bathroom.

She opened the blinds, and then the windows. Sunlight streamed in, accentuating thick layers of dust on the heavy furniture. That same dust had settled on everything else in the space, and she lovingly wiped it away as she packed his clothes and personal items into boxes and taped them shut. She stripped the bedding, trying, not to focus on the person who had recently slept here, and washed it all, then folded each piece into plastic storage bags. She removed the pictures of her parents from the bedroom walls and arranged them in the living room, displayed for all to see. Well, for her to see, mostly. She rarely had visitors. But having her parents watching though the lenses of old photographs made the house feel somehow less empty.

After storing her father's things, she wiped down the furniture and employed all her muscles to drag and shove each heavy piece, rearranging the space so that the bed faced the east window, where she could wake up to the morning sunlight, shining through. A brand new comforter, soft sheets, and frilly pillows finished the transformation—the new items an extravagance that required digging into what little money she had saved, but the end result, wherein she reclaimed control of her life, made the expenditure worth every penny.

When she was finished, she established herself on the couch and ordered takeout seafood to go with her movie, replacing the crab that Caspian once ate, and feeling a sense of self-satisfaction that she'd been missing for a long, long time.

Chapter Sixteen

TIME WITH HIS MOTHER SENT Caspian careening backward, to the days of his childhood and memories of a life that centered on him and his mother, a team of two. She reminded him about the school he'd attended—which explained why he'd picked up on reading so fast—human children he'd played with, medical professionals who had treated him. With her help, he recalled learning to read, beginning to write, to ride a bicycle and skate on wheeled shoes. And how much time they'd spent at the beach.

Every weekend, both Saturday and Sunday, they had staked the same spot at the same beach, where they stayed from sunup, to sundown. Even during the winter months, when the water formed sheets of ice and the winter wind cut through their clothes, his mother had dragged him to the shore, where they built fires in the sand on which they cooked and ate full meals, bundled in blankets and warming their toes over hot coals.

He hadn't known at the time, but learned now that she'd been looking for his father, who left before she'd realized she was expecting, and who she fully believed would return someday. She hadn't counted on him reappearing only long enough to kidnap her son and spirit him away to Atlantis.

After Caspian disappeared, she had continued to spend her time on the beach, waiting, praying, pleading. But now, instead of searching for her long-lost love, she awaited the son of her own flesh. She had never stopped hoping.

Now that Caspian had returned to her, she felt that her life mission was ultimately fulfilled.

"I did, eventually, move on from your father," she explained. "After you'd been gone for nearly two years, I found the courage to date again. I was so lonely, so wrecked by losing you both. Joseph burst into my life like a beacon shining through a storm. He provided me light, and peace, and eventually, another son."

Caspian straightened in the living-room recliner, a cushy chair the same color as sand, but much smoother against his skin. His mother still lived in the home they'd shared when he was small, though it had changed significantly since then. "I have a brother?"

Mother, whose name he'd learned was Mona—which clarified how he'd come to believe her name was momma—sat forward in her own sand-colored chair, covering his hand with hers. "Yes. Some time has passed, Caspian. Your brother has grown, and is now away at college. He's dating a young lady named Cindy—I haven't met her yet, but I already love her because she makes Russell so happy."

Caspian withdrew his hand from his mother's and examined his once-scaly skin, wondering if he and his human brother might look alike. "Might I meet my brother, soon?"

Mona drew in a pained breath, her stone-colored eyes crinkling at the edges. "Perhaps. He has only just left again, and won't likely come home to visit for quite some time."

Hidden truths lay behind Mona's eyes, so Caspian stood, his full height towering over his mother's small, frail frame, and casting a shadow across the dark wood floor. "He does not know of me."

She stood, wringing her hands with anxiety. "I've wanted to tell him since he was old enough to understand—but each time I tried, I couldn't. Why tell a boy that he has a brother he might never know? One he might never be allowed to meet? I've always believed that you would return to me someday—and I am so happy you've finally come—but with each year that passed, I lost more hope. I didn't want Russ to suffer the same expectation, the same hope as me, and then to know the excruciating loss if you never came back."

Caspian ran his hand along the knotted, wooden mantle littered with so many photos—a young boy, he assumed to be Russell, a middle-aged man, the boy and man and his mother together. "Will you tell him about me now?"

Mona picked up the photo of the boy and held it to her chest. "Do you intend to stay?"

He yearned to answer yes, that he would stay and live ashore with her, and his brother, and his beloved Elise, who he missed as a lost part of his soul. The longer he dwelled ashore, the more attached he became to the people here. But he did not know how long the pearl pendant would continue allowing him to breathe.

Even if he chose to give up his throne, his kingdom, at some point, he would be forced to pay a visit to Atlantis and ask Maui to find him a more permanent solution to breathing—but he feared that once he returned home, visiting land a second time would result in an all-out battle. And if he did manage to come back, it would mean severing all ties with his father, and the kingdom he'd grown quite fond of. "I do not yet know if such a thing is possible—there are details that must be seen to, and I—"

Mona crossed the room to a bookshelf, and removed a carved, wooden box. "Tang has such a hold on you. How will I ever convince him to let you go? To allow you to make your own choices, as any grown man should?"

"Mother, it is not only about my father. I am betrothed for a joining. I am intended to rule Atlantis. And I am given a poison that helps me to breathe ashore—but it grows weak, and when it is gone, I shall shrivel and die."

Her watery eyes pierced his, skewering him deeply enough that he took an instinctive step back to create a safe distance between them. "Betrothed to a mermaid you don't like. In a city you have wanted to leave for years. And there are plenty of poisons available here. You tell me what you need, and I'll help you find it."

"I do not believe such a thing possible. This poison comes from a very rare sea creature, and is delivered through the pendant I wear. I do not fully understand how it works, or why, only that the poison causes my gills to be paralyzed for a time, forcing my human lungs to inflate. I must have this thing to live."

She drilled a finger into his chest. "You tell your father that it's *my* turn. I gave you life, and now I get to be part of it. Tell him that if he insists on holding you captive, he better have a face-to-face conversation with me about it. I was weak when I knew him, but I'm much stronger now."

"Father is not kind about such things." He didn't believe that talking to anyone would sway his father's decision, but Mona seemed determined, and confident—if such a thing were possible. "He will not visit the shore to communicate with you."

Calm fell over her face. "Yes, he will. You tell him you found me, and that I demand an audience with the Sea King." She slipped an old-fashioned iron key into the wooden lock and opened the top of the box. The inside had been filled with sparkling, precious gems. She studied the stones as if inspecting their quality, then plucked a large, clear, sparkling one and held it between thumb and forefinger so it refracted a beam of sunlight, showering the room with rainbows. "Give him this. Tell him I will surrender the rest when we meet, face-to-face."

Caspian accepted the offered stone, marveling at its sharp, luminescent beauty. "What is it?"

Mona funneled the rest of the gems into a felt bag and locked them inside the box, then replaced it behind the books on the shelf. "It's a diamond. Valuable and expensive to humans, and a weakness of King Tangaroa. I learned many things about your father that summer when you were conceived. Thievery proved to be a hobby of his, especially when it came to pretty things that humans consider of great value."

Caspian inspected the nugget, closing it in his fist, then opening it again to assure that the sparkle had not faded. "It's so tiny, and not very colorful. Why would my father wish for such an item? It holds no value in Atlantis."

Mona laughed, leading Caspian into the kitchen. "Oh, I know. He didn't even know what he was stealing until I pointed out how much trouble he would be in if he were to get caught. Somehow, that only seemed to fuel him to collect more sparkly baubles."

Caspian tested the weight in the gem, and the size, and understood that this tiny stone could support someone like Elise for quite a long time. "Where does one gather such things? Where did you find them?"

Mona led him into the kitchen and dug into the fridge for ingredients, setting each item on the counter. "One would gather them in a mine, or more likely, a jewelry store or supplier. But I got these from your father. Kept them hidden for all these years. I suppose Tang's forgotten about his stash, but perhaps he'll remember, once you show him that larger one."

"My father gave them to you? Why would he do such a thing if he desired them for himself?" Having learned a bit about chopping and cooking while living with Elise, Caspian located a cutting board and took on the task of peeling and chopping the potatoes his mother had set out.

Mona slid a frying pan onto the stove and lit the flame, placing two portions of meat inside and dousing both with spices and oil. "To be honest, I don't know as much about your father as I thought I did—back when I was young and stupid. The best thing I can tell

148

you is the conclusions I've come to in my own mind—after years and years of mulling over what I knew then, mixed with what I've learned over years of research. As I understand, human jewels are illegal in Atlantis. And for whatever reason, your father amassed quite a collection, anyway. In fact, on what turned out to be the last day that I would see him, Tang and I decided to have a cookout on the beach where we'd met. He was always willing to eat his fish raw—something I never understood—but I simply couldn't stomach it. Especially since, as I later learned, I was expecting you." She glanced up, a smile warming her face before she refocused on cooking. "We built a fire, and he waded out to see what fish he could catch. By this time, I didn't question his ability, as he'd proven himself more than able, time and again. We only ever ate seafood, and he never bothered with removing skin or shells—I suppose that's one of many clues I should have picked up on."

Caspian swept the potatoes into a bowl, and transferred them to Mona, who traded him for the makings of a salad. "Thank you darling. You've become so good at human cooking."

"You are welcome, Mother."

"Anyway," she continued. "He usually carried a woven bag around with him, but he left the bag with me while he fished, and I was curious. I was so hopelessly in love with him by that time, and I knew so little about him. I thought perhaps I would find—well, to be honest, I'm not sure what I expected to find. Perhaps a driver's license or car keys or anything that might connect him to Oceanside. Instead, I ended up with a handful of stolen gems, and multiple articles of clothing—straight off the racks of a nearby store."

"My father was a thief?" Caspian chopped the remainder of the lettuce and brushed it into the bowl that Mona had provided. "This does not seem correct to me."

She turned from the stove, picking up a second knife and joining Caspian in chopping. "I know. It didn't seem right to me, either. Even with the ink-tags attached, I couldn't comprehend that he had stolen every last bit of it. Anyway, as I went through his bag, Tang hollered that he'd caught us some crabs—which was my signal to stir the coals in our little fire so he could drop them into it. I shoved the clothes back in the bag and pocketed the gems—determined to ask him about them later. Unfortunately, later turned out to mean many years down the road."

"When he came to take me." Caspian set his knife aside, mind reeling with this unknown side of his supposedly respectable father.

Mona nodded, added cucumbers into the salad and then picked up a tomato. "Yes. He showed up to retrieve his treasure, and saw you, recognized you as his own, and rather than giving me an opportunity to go home and fetch the gems, he took you and left. I have not seen him since."

"I was far more valuable to him than rocks."

"You were. Though, part of me will always wonder if he would have left you, had I been able to produce his treasure on the spot." Finished chopping, Mona placed the used dishes in the sink and wiped the remaining juices off the counter.

"No," Caspian said, his voice faint while sound roared in his ears. "I do not believe he could have left me behind. My father—he is very traditional, and in Atlantis, having an heir is the only way to preserve one's necessary presence as royalty. I simply cannot imagine that the Sea King would have allowed me to remain with my mother, whether you had access to his treasure or not."

Mona stroked the side of his face with the backs of her fingers. "No, he wouldn't. I believe you're right about that. Anyway, the point is, all this time, I've saved those gems for him. No matter how tempted I was to sell them and use the money to support us, and then later my husband and Russ—I've never been able to do it, because part of me has always known I'd need them someday. For this. I will use them to help you find your way back to me, to help you stay with me, if you want. It's the only reason I didn't sell these jewels long ago, during far too many lean years."

Caspian drew back, again, unable to make a promise he might not be able to keep. "Mother, I . . ."

"I know." She dropped her hand and moved to the stove to flip the sizzling meat. "You have a life in Atlantis. A future. All you have here is your past, and I understand that. But even if you choose to go back, I'll always be here for you. I'll always do whatever I can to clear a path, to do whatever is necessary to allow you to at least visit from time-to-time."

Something in his chest quivered. This woman who—only weeks ago—he'd hardly known, was now willing to set aside everything she had, in order to spend time with him. No promises, no obligations— only hope for more. More of everything she could get. Just as Elise had been. Was this how it felt to be loved? "Thank you, Mother. I would enjoy meeting my brother and knowing more of my human family."

At the mention of his brother, Mona stiffened, concentrating more fully on preparing the food. "Well. As I said, your brother may not come around for a while. If you're able to stick around until he does, of course you'll meet him."

Caspian had never known a sibling. The idea that one existed excited him, and at the same time crowded him with dread. "How long might that be?"

"Oh, I don't know." She waved a hand in the air as if the details were unimportant—but Caspian knew better. His mother had waited for him for more than twenty years. Of course she knew when she could expect another visit from her human son. She continued, "I thought maybe he'd be home for the Labor Day weekend, but he called last night to let me know that he'll be working, and unable to make the drive. It'll be weeks before he has another chance."

"Perhaps you could inform him that he is needed here?" Caspian suggested, knowing before he said it what the answer would be.

"I'll see what I can do, but you have to understand, my son, that college is very important. It's a high-pressure place for your brother. He can't skip class, or leave work, so, a visit from him is unlikely for a while."

"Very well." *Then I shall stay until he does.* The second full moon of his visit had come and gone, leaving Caspian certain that his allotted time ashore had already run out. He was now on borrowed time. "Perhaps after our meal you will allow me to show you my cove—the place where I first came ashore."

Mona turned, pinning him with a gaze of delight. "Of course, my son. Definitely.

Chapter Seventeen

CASPIAN'S OLD BEDROOM HAD BEEN taken over by the younger brother he'd never met, all evidence that Caspian had ever lived there either erased, or buried beneath a lifetime of childhood loves and successes, including a wide shelf filled with academic achievement certificates and sports trophies, apparently earned by Russell.

From the day he'd left Elise and moved to his mother's home, Caspian had longed to meet this boy, this man, who should have been part of his life and his childhood. He wanted to know so many things about this person, and yet part of him ached for his own loss—for the time he'd missed with his mother, time that someone else had superseded. Beads of jealousy tumbled around inside him. He could not remember experiencing such feelings since he'd last been human, and very small, when a playmate received a toy that Caspian coveted—one he'd wished to steal, had he been able.

He remembered planning to punch the boy in the back, but his mother had stopped him, having seen the calculations in her son's every move. "No, no, Caspian," she'd said. "We don't *ever* hurt another person for having something that we wish was ours. It's human nature to desire things that don't belong to us, but we must never, ever want something so badly that we would willingly hurt another to receive it."

He remembered the discussion now, sitting on the edge of the bed in a room that looked nothing like he remembered it. Pictures and writings and a collection of figurines that all appeared to go together in a game of make-believe—none of it belonged to him, and Caspian envied the boy who was raised by his—their—mother.

Preparing for bed was a comfort, as Mona had, in her wisdom, purchased a variety of clothing and toiletries for Caspian before his arrival, as if she'd known that he would not have the coverings he needed for human living. This saved him from having to wear clothing that belonged to someone else, allowing him to form a sense of pride in owning personal human possessions. Once he'd brushed his teeth and donned his soft, flannel pajamas, Caspian lay atop the bed, still unable to get used to sleeping covered up. He found the weight uncomfortable and restraining.

On the nightstand sat a stack of books that Mona had brought in—books he remembered from childhood. He'd been able to read them before he left human life to become one of the Mer. He picked up one with bright pictures on the cover, and flipped through the pages, proud to note that entire words now jumped off the pages without much effort—truly, his memory worked at a remarkable pace since he'd come here. But tonight, he was not in the mood to practice reading, so he flicked the switch on the bedside lamp and closed his eyes, attempting to drift to sleep, now that the sun had gone down.

He'd taken to sleeping on Mona's schedule, which was very different from the sleep schedule he'd had with Elise. That is, when they'd slept. He still had not told his mother of Elise, and he wasn't sure if he should. Too much about his time here muddled his brain with confusion, longing, and ache, and so he attempted to close Elise into a box and store her away in a far corner of his heart. The task was proving more difficult than he first anticipated.

Sometime later, footsteps dragged him out of slumber, followed by the turning knob on his bedroom door. Caspian sat up, confused when the shadowy figure appeared much taller and broader than Mona. "Hello?" he said, praying that his father had not found him yet. He was not prepared to return to Atlantis in the dead of night.

The overhead light flared, illuminating a man standing in the doorway. He had hair of a similar color to Caspian's, and shoulders nearly as wide—though not quite. He stood of a slender build, scrawny and undernourished, and his green eyes narrowed, his face screwed up with anger and hatred. "What are you doing in *my* mother's house?" he demanded. "Who are you?"

His mother's house? Caspian stood, allowing his brawny, muscular frame to overshadow the other man's. "This house belongs to *my* mother," he explained. "She has allowed me to abide here until I am required to return home to my father's land. I am Caspian of—" He cut himself off before giving away too much. "I am Caspian."

"Who? What are you doing in my room? If my mother let you stay here, she would have told me." The young man advanced, hands balled into fists as if he believed himself capable of overpowering Caspian, but Caspian stood his ground. "Are you some kind of squatter? Taking advantage of a vulnerable woman?"

"*Your* room?" Caspian allowed the words to circle in his head, his attention falling on a photograph, propped on top of the dresser. The young man in that photograph appeared younger, shorter, scrawnier, but the face, the eyes, were the same. "You are Russell?"

Russell fell back a step, anger melting into confusion. "How do you know my name? Who are you? I'm so confused right now."

Only hours ago, Caspian had longed to meet the man who was his brother. Now, as he faced the angry person on the other side of the room, jealousy reared up, threatening to take over. "Our mother told me of you," he said. "That you have chosen to leave her, and that you are unable to visit often."

Russell rolled his eyes and covered his face with his hands before shoving those hands through his unruly mass of short hair. "Is that what this is? Her sick attempt to guilt me into moving home and doing my classes online? This is ridiculous. I don't know who you are, but I'm an only child—always have been. Whatever my mom's paying you to help her guilt me, I'll make sure you get it. But only if you leave quietly, and right now."

This was not how Caspian had imagined his first meeting with his brother would go. "I cannot leave now." He drooped onto the bed. "I have not yet remembered all the things I came to learn. And I have not said goodbye to Mother. I promised her that, this time, I would not leave without her knowledge. Therefore, I am unable to do as you ask, brother, and for that, I am sorry."

Russell snatched the desk chair and pulled it with him until it pinned Caspian's knees, then he dropped into it. "Okay, let's start this over. Tell me who you are and what you're doing here. No more evading. Tell me now, and I might be convinced to forgo calling the police."

Caspian held out a hand, as he'd learned was customary for human men. "I am Caspian of Atlantis, son of the Merman Sea King, Tangaroa, and the human woman with whom he once joined, and whose name is Mona Harris. I was born of a woman too young, and stolen from her grasp in my sixth year, forced below the sea, to the city of Atlantis, where I reign as Prince, someday to become the new Sea King."

Russell blinked, his lips quirking. "I get it. So, um, Caspian—was it?" Caspian nodded his approval, and Russell continued. "Uh, where did my mother find you . . . exactly? By any chance, have you recently spent time in a mental hospital?"

Caspian had experienced a variety of amused condescension when he'd worked at the resort, so he understood from the undertones that Russell still did not believe him. "Mona, our mother, sought me out in a restaurant where my . . . A beach restaurant where I used to spend time." He opened the nightstand drawer and withdrew the note that he'd kept, offering it to Russell. "I had come ashore to find her, and as I searched for her, so did she search for me."

Russell stared at the paper, scrutinizing it as if hoping to find something more than what was written.

Finally, he reverted his attention to Caspian's face. "Okay, I don't know how you conned my mother into writing this—it's definitely her handwriting—but you're a sick man. A dead one, if you've come here to scam or otherwise hurt her."

Confused at the anger that raged within his brother, Caspian removed from the drawer a single photograph his mother had kept of the two of them. "I do not know what is a con, or a scam. I only know that *your* mother is also mine. She is the woman whose arms I have longed for since I was taken in my sixth year."

Russell accepted the picture, the blood draining from his face as he stood from the chair. "How is this possible? I don't understand. If this is true—and I'm not saying I believe it, but if so—how have I never heard of you? Never known your name? Why would she not tell me that she had another son?"

Caspian turned his face toward the window, where the light of a crescent moon sneaked through the blinds. "I do not believe she ever expected me to return. However she hoped, she could not know if this day would come. I do not understand why she has not spoken of me, but my father caused her great pain. Perhaps she hoped to shield you from the agony of uncertainty." Hearing his own words, Caspian thought of Elise, realizing with a flash that this same type of uncertainty might be why she had kept his mother's

160

information from him. Perhaps she had been afraid of what would happen when his mother was found.

Russell dropped onto the bed next to Caspian, his eyes haunted, hands shaking. "That's a pretty damn big secret to keep from your kid."

"It is a damn big secret to keep from everyone," Caspian murmured, mimicking his brother's tone. "I cannot imagine the loneliness she has endured for all these years."

Russell challenged his brother, his face hardening again. "Okay, so assuming I believed the whole long-lost brother thing, uh, Sea King? Atlantis. Wives tales. I don't believe any of that, and never have. Let's try for the truth, now."

Caspian unbuttoned his flannel pajama shirt and withdrew his pearl pendant, exposing it to his brother. "The legends are true. All of them. This pendant was created by my cousin Maui, a Mer scientist and experimenter. He believed that a half-human Mer could have his or her human lungs restored through a poison, which would allow us to reside, temporarily, on land. I am half human, and this is the source of my breath."

Russell shook his head, still in denial. "My mother and a Sea King? I'm still having a hard time believing any of it. Where did you say this Atlantis was located?"

"It is far below the darkest depth of the blue sea, protected by barriers, and hidden in tunnels. When I left my home, this was the shore nearest to our borders."

"This is crazy. I just . . . I'm in shock even talking about it. Feels surreal." Russell stared at the picture of his mother and Caspian, his eyes jetting back and forth between Caspian's face and the printed photo. "How can I be sure that this is you? It could be anyone."

Caspian pressed his finger to the photo, pointing out the slits on the boy's neck, then pressed that same finger to his own. "Gills."

Balling his free hand into a fist, Russell inspected the picture, then the lines on Caspian's neck, then the picture again. "Not enough," he proclaimed.

As a last offering, Caspian stood and retrieved a leather pouch from the desk, then returned to his spot next to Russell and took his brother's fisted hand, smoothing it flat. The jewels he'd salvaged for Elise tumbled into Russell's palm, sparkling in a rainbow of colors. "I gathered these from the remnants of a sunken ship. I do not believe this is something easy to purchase, or steal, in this land."

Russell blinked in disbelief, shifting the stones around in his hand. "No, not easy. At all. You know, you're going to get robbed. This is like millions of dollars' worth of stones, right here."

The number meant nothing to Caspian so he shrugged, opening the pouch so Russell could replace them. Elise would not keep them when he left, but he had brought them for her, and intended to hide them until she was prepared to accept them.

For the first time, Russell faced Caspian, his eyes searching for familiarity, for truth. Whatever he found must have satisfied his remaining doubts, because he returned the photograph to Caspian and fell back on the bed, rubbing his forehead. "How long have you been here?"

Since he'd left Elise, he had not returned to his job at the resort, and with Mona's different sleep schedule, the nights and days had blurred together, making it impossible for him to keep track. "Days, only."

"And how long do you plan to stick around?"

Caspian glanced at the sliver of moonlight sneaking past the window blinds, feeling the pressure of time running short. "I've been ashore too long already, I'm afraid. I am soon to be joined, and I fear my father or my betrothed will soon demand my return."

Russell propped himself up on one elbow, facing Caspian. "You're engaged?"

Caspian chewed on his lips the way Elise had done during the times they fought. "Only in the eyes of my father and the city of Atlantis. I do not wish to marry the mermaid to whom I am promised. I do not love her."

"Why don't you just tell your father that? Surely he can understand."

My *father could not understand something such as love.*
He knew this now, having met his mother and learned
the agony the Sea King had put her through—twice.
"The Mer do not understand much of love," Caspian
explained. "They are a practical people, concerned
more with living in peace and ensuring the survival of
the species, than with carnal feelings or those of the
heart. I did not know much of love myself, until I came
ashore."

To this, Russell tipped his head, sitting up further.
"That look in your eyes makes me feel like you're not
talking about how much you love your mom."

This time it was Caspian who fell against the
pillows, eyes squeezed shut as pain lanced his chest. "I
am not."

"Bro, how long have you been here? And by here, I
mean . . . in town."

"Two full moon cycles, and halfway into a third."

Russell blew out a long, slow breath. "But you've
only been here with my mom for a few days?"

Caspian popped open one eye. "Our mom. And
yes."

"Wha—what did you do in between?"

He opened the second eye, surprised to find that
both felt strangely wet. "I learned to love a woman."

164

Neither of the brothers slept that night, having far too much to catch up on, and both worried that their time would be cut short. Russell because of the need to return to school, and Caspian, because he knew he was already on borrowed time. When the first pink rays of sun peeked through the blinds, replacing the faded, gray moonlight, both men slept with the knowledge that each had a brother—however reluctant they were to acknowledge the connection. Caspian shared with Russell everything about his time with Elise, miserable with the memories of how he'd left, and confused as to why his joints ached and his chest felt heavy every time he thought of her. Which was always.

Russell regaled Caspian with tales about growing up in Oceanside, attending school and how he'd always felt like something important was missing from his life. Something he couldn't name. He spoke of a woman back at school, whom he'd been dating for quite some time, and had considered asking to marry him. And he admitted that he'd come home seeking advice from their mother. But by morning, the men agreed that, for whatever reason, Mona had kept them a secret from each other. Under the circumstances, they decided that perhaps it was best that Mona not know Russell had come at all. At least, not this time.

Though his eyes blurred with exhaustion, Caspian's brain spun with information and hope. He had a family here in Oceanside. Not simply a ruler father who kept him as an heir and assigned caregivers to raise him, but a mother who had never stopped looking for him, never stopped missing him, and a brother who hadn't known he existed, yet who had already accepted him as family. And Elise—according to Russell, if Caspian could find a way to remain ashore indefinitely, there was no reason why he couldn't also keep Elise for a mate—or in human terms, a wife. All he had to do was give up his throne.

In the moment, the throne of Atlantis felt like such a trivial sacrifice when compared to his experience with love, and his newfound connection to family.

Late into the morning, Caspian crept from his bedroom—or Russell's bedroom, now—for a trip to the bathroom, and afterward made a detour to the kitchen to search for food as his stomach rumbled with hunger.

Mona met him in the doorway, plate of cold pancakes in hand. "I was just on my way to your room to check on you," she said, her voice cheery with happiness. "Are you feeling all right? You've slept for an awfully long time."

Caspian shuffled into the kitchen, knowing that Mona would follow. "I did not sleep well in the night, but got some this morning. Is this breakfast for me?" He nodded at the plate in Mona's hand, and she set it on the table in front of him. "Yes. I was just debating

166

whether or not I should throw them away and start over. Would you like fresh ones? I can make more."

Caspian shook his head, dumping a generous helping of syrup on the cakes, as his new addiction to this thing called sugar continued to grow. "These will be lovely, thank you."

Mona sat in the chair across from him, resting her chin on her hand and staring as he ate. When he was halfway through the cakes, she asked, "What would you like to do today? We could go shopping and buy you more clothes and supplies. Or we can visit the park you liked as a child. Have you seen a movie yet? We could do that and maybe have lunch or dinner? Or both." She reached out her hand to rest on his forearm. "I'm just so pleased to have you here, I'm not quite sure what to do next."

As much as he longed to make more memories with his mother, Russell only had this one day. By morning, he would return to his life further inland, at a place Caspian could not picture, but that he imagined was far away. "Actually, Mother, there is something I wish to take care of today. You see, I had a job at the resort before I found you, and I would like to make amends with those whom I have let down. Perhaps we might act on your plans tomorrow? I should love to join you, then."

The crease on Mona's forehead scrunched in disbelief. "All right. I can certainly drive you to the resort for that. Shouldn't take long, and then we can cross something else off our list."

Again, Caspian longed to ride around with his mother, to show her off as a trophy because it had been so long since he had a mother, he needed to express his happiness in having been reunited with her. But Russell—he'd promised. And he may not have another chance to spend time with his brother. "I am sorry, Mother. This is something I must do alone."

Mona's hand on his arm squeezed tight enough to cause discomfort. "Caspian. You can't swim. They'll take you back, force you away from me, and we're only just beginning to know each other again. Please don't leave before you've given me a chance."

Caspian set his fork aside and covered her hand with his. "I do not intend to swim, and I will not allow the Mer to force me home without first informing you, I promise. Leaving is far from my intention today."

"How will you get around? Find your way?"

Russell had warned him that their mother would question his independence, and had coached him on the correct answers. "Perhaps you can write down the address so that if I become lost, I might hire a car and get home that way. Mother, please understand that this is important to me."

Mona stood, swallowing any further objections as she retrieved her purse from a cabinet near the door. She withdrew several green bills and set them in front

168

of him. "You're going to need this, just in case. You can buy food with it, or drinks, or get a ride on any public transportation." Next, she wrote the requested numbers on a sheet of paper, and gave him that as well. "Please, promise me you'll return tonight. I can't bear to lose you again. Not yet."

"I promise." Finally, a promise he could keep.

By the time he returned to his room, Russell had showered and dressed, and cleaned up any evidence that he'd been there. "How'd it go?"

Caspian handed his brother the bills. "I believe it went well. She intends to visit a neighbor friend and help care for some animals while I'm away."

Russell shoved some clothes into his brother's arms. "Fantastic. Now, get dressed. Our first priority this morning is to do something about your hair. I've never known anyone more in need of a cut and style. And a good shampoo. We'll take care of that first, and then head to the mall and get you a club-worthy outfit. Later tonight, I vote we go to Coco Cabana for drinks and live music. One of my friends is a member of the cover band that plays there sometimes—I'd love to introduce you."

"I should like Elise to be there," Caspian said, remembering the first time he'd visited the bar and all the events that followed. Just thinking about her caused his body to react, and his pulse to quicken.

"Perhaps we can call her work and invite her to also attend?"

Russell shook his head. "No can do, my friend. Makes you come across as desperate. But we can call one of her friends, let them in on the secret. Did you ever meet any of her friends?"

Caspian considered the other waitresses at the Turtle and decided on Shelley. "I believe I know a person who might be helpful, yes."

Russell clapped his hands together. "Excellent. Let's go."

They arrived at the club while the band was setting up, and Caspian immediately claimed the table he had once shared with Elise. Perhaps this was because he missed her so, or because nerves coiled inside him as if on the cusp of exploding. Or maybe it was simply about showing her that he remembered every moment of their time together, treasured it, and that he hoped to have more, if it became possible.

Russell waved a waitress to the table, and she soon returned, carrying four drinks in triangular shaped glasses. Caspian struggled to keep his eyes from the door, biting his lip and scuffing the toe of his shiny new shoes on the floor. "Relax," Russell told him. "She'll be here soon."

"What if she does not come? What if Shelley is unable to persuade her?"

Russell shoved a cocktail into his brother's hand. "Drink this. It'll calm your nerves."

Caspian inspected the pink liquid in the clear glass, deciding it reminded him of Paihana, a mind-altering substance that had recently become popular in Atlantis, specifically among those who could afford the luxury. He accepted the beverage and downed it in three swallows, choking afterward because the cool liquid somehow burned in his throat. "Gah, what is this vile formula?"

Russell laughed. "A mixture of several things. The one that burns is called Vodka." He lowered his voice and leaned closer to Caspian. "Technically, I'm not old enough to purchase this variety of drinks, but that's what fake ID's are for."

Caspian set the glass down, squeezing his eyes and nose and forehead in distaste, and then snatched a second glass, deciding that a bit of extra courage couldn't be a bad thing. "I have heard that word before. What is an ID?"

Russell brought out a wallet from his pocket, and removed a smooth, slim card with his picture on it. "Looks like this. It tells the world that I'm allowed to drive, and it has my age and birthdate and basic physical features in case I change drastically from the picture. Lots of businesses require these when you buy something with a credit card."

He thought back to his time at the resort and the slim cards the customers used to pay for drinks and food and other services, and concluded that those cards were the credit ones to which Russell referred. "Might I be allowed to procure an ID?"

Russell put his license away with a shrug. "I don't know. Guess it depends on if my mom has a birth certificate for you." After another second of thought, he removed a second one to show Caspian. "This is the fake one. Pretty much the exact same, except we changed the year on the birthdate. We could buy you one of these, if you want."

Caspian grinned, feeling more like a human with each day that passed, and especially on this one that he'd spent with his brother. "I would like that very much," he decided, wondering how long he could pose as a human, and if he might truly be able to stay in Oceanside indefinitely. "It might come in handy if I find a new job, as mother would want."

Russell tapped his glass against Caspian's. "I'll give my guy a call tonight, see about expediting the process. If you're wanting to look for a job, having ID is going to be crucial."

Russell continued to speak, but Caspian's attention directed across the room. Shelley and Elise pushed through the crowd, sidling up to the bar, where Shelley slapped down some money and shouted over the noise as the music roared to life. Caspian's brother stopped speaking mid-sentence, his attention following Caspian's.

"That's them?"

Caspian nodded, unable to speak around his thick tongue.

"Which one's Elise?"

She'd worn a light, flimsy dress that ruffled with every movement, outlining her slim, curvy attributes. The white fabric fluttered around her knees as she slid onto a barstool and leaned her elbows on the counter, her dark, red hair waving gently over her shoulders and falling halfway down her back. From what he could tell, she appeared thinner, her skin drawn tight over her forehead and cheeks, and her eyes more hollow. And still, her beauty outshone every being—human or Mer—Caspian had ever encountered, including the Spanish Dancing Jellyfish, whose rings of glowing color had always fascinated him, and whose movements flowed and fluttered with more grace than any other creature below the sea.

With shaking fingers, he lifted the second drink to his lips, desperate for something to wet his mouth. "The female sitting on the stool." He gulped the entire contents of the glass in one long swig.

Russell responded with a high, tight whistle. "Yep. Not hard to understand why you'd want to consider staying here instead of going home."

Caspian's attention snapped to his brother. "I did not say such a thing."

"Didn't have to." Russell finished his drink as well, his eyes fixed on the girls across the room. "Listen, I'm not going to tell you what to do, but I am going to give you a word of advice, man-to-man. Because we're brothers."

A male at the bar leaned close to Elise, speaking, and her answering laugh reached Caspian's ears, despite all other sounds, music, voices, clinking glasses, footsteps—everything else competing with the one melodious sound. "What would you do if you were forced to make such a choice?" Caspian asked.

Russell met his brother's gaze, sympathy shining in his green eyes as he clapped Caspian on the shoulder. "Hard call, brother. To be honest—if she loves you, if you're sure, I'd consider sticking around. Women like her just don't appear in a man's life very often. I don't know what the dynamic is like where you're from, but I've dated a lot of women. A lot. Cindy is the first one who has ever meant enough to me that I would introduce her to Mom. She's the first—the only—woman who has forced me to look into the future and consider making more permanent plans. She's a rare breed, my Cindy. And from what you've told me, and what I can see with my own eyes, Elise is too."

Caspian stared into his glass, unable to process the storm of feelings swirling within him. "How do you know?"

"Look at her. She's uncomfortable here, but determined. It's like she wants to move on from you, but can't do it yet. Caspian." Russell waited until Caspian's focus returned to his brother. "She's in love with you. If you love her back, you should hold onto that. Love is a rare treasure that should never be taken for granted. More precious than gold, or silver, or pearls, or . . . anything else. There might never be another person who stirs you the way she does. Are you willing to risk having to live without that feeling in your life? Are you willing to risk losing her?"

When put in such a way, Caspian attempted to imagine his life one year from now. Two years. Ten. Twenty. He imagined himself old and gray and wrinkled, sitting on the porch of a home like his mother's—only his own. None of his visions, his hopes, involved returning to Atlantis. None involved Marietta or his father or the kingdom he was supposed to rule someday. Every dream of his future involved staying on land and being with Elise.

The music tempo changed, swinging into something melancholy and sweet, slower than the high-energy dancing music they'd been playing. He set the glass on the table and stood, refusing to take his eyes from his beloved. "No. I cannot. I will not. Thank you, brother. You have been helpful in many ways this day, and I will forever treasure our time."

Russell grinned, setting his glass aside as well. "Ask her to dance. I'll run interference with the friend. What's her name again?"

"Shelley." Caspian had already begun to move, striding across the dancefloor, through couples and groups, past wait staff carrying trays of drinks, through the middle of two men arguing, until he'd reached Elise, whose shoulder he tapped.

Elise whirled, eyes wide with surprise. "Caspian."

He held out a hand, hoping, praying she would take it. "Would you dance with me?"

She swallowed, accepting his hand and slipping off the stool with a nearly imperceptible nod.

Caspian steered her to the dancefloor, swinging her into his arms the way his brother had showed him in the dressing room, until he held her against his body, pressing closer as desperation and desire clawed inside him—begging to be freed.

"You cut your hair." Her hand skimmed up his neck to touch the newly-shorn edges below his hairline.

He bent his head closer, wondering what it would take to get her to close the distance between her lips and his neck. "Yes. My brother, Russell, claimed it would make me look more human—though I am not

176

sure how to behave with so little protection on my head."

"Your brother?"

"Yes. I have a brother. He is grown, and attends school somewhere far away. He has come to visit only for today." Disappointed when Elise stayed just rigid enough to keep inches of distance between them, Caspian tried again, this time, offering his shoulder.

"Oh. How are you getting along with your mother?" She pulled back, tipping her face up so she could see his.

"She is wonderful." He tilted his closer, desperate for her lips to touch any part of him, even if it was his chin. "Together, we are filling in memories of my past. It is very healing to my heart."

She cleared her throat as if it were clogged. "That's good to hear. I'm glad you've found her, and your answers."

She missed a step, and Caspian stumbled over her foot. "I am sorry, beloved. Have I hurt you?"

Elise blinked, pain shimmering in her eyes. "Not my foot. I can't feel my body anymore, anyway."

"Why?" Tired of the distance between them, he pulled her against his chest and lifted her until her feet dangled above his as they moved.

She blinked rapidly, and swallowed. "Do you really want to talk about this now? Can't we just dance, without bringing up all of life's complications?"

Emotion welled in Caspian, feelings bigger than any he'd experienced before, a storm of pain and love and anguish and joy and desire and familiarity and want. Holding her felt right, it felt free. Being with Elise gave him the strength to swim for his life until he reached the shore. The strength to make a choice he never expected would be a choice at all.

She clung to him, her arms tight around his neck and shoulders, body pressed against his as it had been when they'd loved before, as if she couldn't let go any easier than he could. When the song concluded and a faster, quicker tempo picked up, Caspian set Elise on her feet, but didn't let her go until she drew away saying, "Thank you. I needed that."

"As did I," he croaked. "Elise, might we speak? Perhaps outside? Near the water."

Immediately, her eyes flicked toward the resort. "Okay."

He took her hand, and she let him, and hope surged, overriding his nerves. Once they'd escaped the crowd, he drew her toward the sea, where the waves drown out the sound of voices and laughter and joy, creating a bubble of peace. Uncertain how to begin such a conversation, and not even positive what he wished to say, Caspian faced Elise, frustrated that his tongue felt thick and heavy and somehow just wrong.

Elise blinked, squeezing his fingers. "Did you have something to say?"

178

Caspian coughed, his brain drawing a blank for words. "I . . . how are you? I've missed our time together."

"Surviving." She had to work hard to swallow, and her eyes squeezed shut. "I've missed it, too. I've missed you. But I'm so confused right now. Caspian, why are you here? With me?"

The urge to touch her reared up, and he brushed the backs of his fingers down the side of her jaw. "You are my beloved. I needed to see you, to feel you in my arms."

A sob wrenched from her chest, deep, gutted, as if she'd held it in for weeks and his words had somehow broken it free. "How can you say that? You're still here, your time is limited, and yet I haven't even heard from you for weeks. You don't call, you don't visit, nothing. It's like the moment you found your mother, I stopped existing for you. I realize that you needed time with her, and I'm not saying you had to introduce the two of us right away, but if you truly loved me, you would at least keep in touch. Let me know how things are going—something. Anything."

Air and emotions clogged his throat, making it difficult for him to respond, but he coughed to clear it away. "Elise, I am not accustomed to human courting practice. I did not understand these things."

She whirled toward the sea, turning her back on him. "It's not just a human courting practice, Caspian.

It's . . . When you love someone, truly love them, it shouldn't be easy to walk away—under any circumstances. When you love someone, you miss them, every minute of every day and all through the night. You can't get them out of your mind, and your chest feels heavy from the pressure when they're not close. When you love someone, you find a way to be with them, despite impossible circumstances. To my knowledge, you have done none of those things, felt none of those things. I'm not your beloved—I'm your be-liked. Or your summer fling, or your . . . first, I guess. I don't know."

Her shoulders slumped in defeat as his hands wrapped around them, pulling her backward into his body, and then wrapping his arms across her chest. "Elise, there are many reasons why you have not seen or heard from me, but my feelings for you have not changed. They will never change. I have a brother, and he has helped me to understand what I must do. He has brought me here to teach me how to woo you."

She laughed, turning in his arms. "Woo me?"

"That is what he said. I do not fully understand what the word means."

Her smile faltered, and the shadow returned to her eyes. "Listen. I can appreciate the sentiment. I really can. And you know I'll take all the time with you that I can get before you leave, but I'm not a boomerang. You can't throw me away, and then bring me back, only to throw me out again. My heart's not strong enough for that."

"Beloved, I do not wish to throw you out at all. I wish to keep you."

A tear broke free and ran down her cheek. "I wish you could keep me, too. But we both know you're going home soon. I don't know how to deal with that."

He *was* going home. Had to. If he were to have any hope of remaining alive and living ashore, he must first inform his father, and then ask Maui to resupply his pendant with the poison that kept him breathing. "I am. But I shall return, my love."

Another tear fell, followed by another. Elise sniffled and drew away from him. "When? In five years? Ten? Twenty? Caspian, you've told me yourself that time is measured differently in Atlantis. If you have a brother who's giving you dating advice, then you must've been gone at least twenty years. What am I supposed to do in the meantime? Wait?" She continued to back away from him, her steps gaining momentum over the sand. "I don't know how to do that. I can't be alone for the next twenty years on the hope that *maybe* you'll come back."

Caspian could not give her an answer because she was correct. Time was measured differently in Atlantis, and there was no guarantee that his father would accept his intensions happily. In fact, Caspian felt quite certain that he would encounter quite a degree of opposition. As much as he wanted to, he still could not make her a promise, not until he was sure he would be able to keep it. His heart ached with sorrow. "You must not wait, my love. Not if I am gone long. But please allow me . . ."

She shook her head. "I can't. I can't have this conversation right now. I need to go home. Please tell Shelley I'm sorry." She turned and ran up the sand, past the building and straight to the parking lot, where she climbed into one of the cabs waiting in the line.

Stunned, and sick to his stomach, Caspian returned to the bar, where Russell and Shelley had engaged in lively conversation. Russell saw Caspian approaching and stood, waving him over. "This is my brother," Russell told Shelley. "Still sounds so strange to me. I have a brother. But it's also cool. Like a built-in best friend."

Shelley frowned, her eyes taking in Caspian's face, and then searching the rest of the club. "Where's Elise?"

Caspian could only shake his head. "She said to tell you she's sorry. She's gone home."

Shelley stood, eyes narrowed. "What did you say to her? What did you do?"

"I called her my beloved, and I tried to explain . . . but I have failed her. I can see that now. And I must make it right." Desperation clawed at his insides, his throat, stomach, chest, as he clasped Russell's arm. "Help me make it right."

Shelley followed Caspian and Russell out to the parking lot. "Was she sick again? She still hasn't fully recovered from that nasty virus she had last month."

"I do not believe so," Caspian murmured. "Only angry. Always angry."

"You can't blame her," Shelley pointed out. "You did live with her for almost two months, and then one day just up and leave. Of course she's guarded. And yes, angry. Who wouldn't be?"

Russell glanced at his watch. "Listen. I really do have to get back to school tomorrow, but maybe you should go to her work, bring her flowers, some kind of sparkly gift, and then tell her how you feel."

"I tried to tell her, but failed."

Russell shook his head, rolling his eyes. "I'll help you write it down, then. At this point, you have nothing to lose. It's either go big or go home, and I say you go big."

"But I must also go home," Caspian reminded him. "I must purchase an amount of poison that will allow me to breathe for the span of Elise's life, and I must get it in Atlantis."

Shelley blinked. "Um, what now?"

Russell squeezed his brother's arm and stomped on his foot. "Figure of speech. Family thing. Never mind, him. He's not from here." He took down Shelley's number and paid a cab driver to take her home, then glared at Caspian. "Getting careless, don't you think?"

Caspian dropped onto a bench, head in his hands. "I can no longer control my tongue. I do not understand it."

Russell laughed, sitting next to him. "That's love for you. Don't worry, though. I'm told that speaking through it gets easier with time."

Chapter Eighteen

ELISE DRAGGED HERSELF OUT OF bed, face swollen and puffy from spending the night crying—again. She didn't know when she'd become such a weepy-baby. She hadn't even shed so many tears when her father died, and Caspian had only been part of her life for two short months.

Gloriously happy months that she would never, ever forget, because his loss would ache forever.

She should've known better than to go out with Shelley. The girl had such an idyllic view of life, such a zest and zeal for music and dance and alcohol, so when she'd invited Elise for a girl's night out, Elise had agreed, simply because she needed *something. Someone.* Anything had to be better than staying home alone and pining, staring at the phone and hoping Caspian would call.

They had made memories in every part of this house, and those memories haunted her, kept her awake at night, and occupied her daily thoughts. She'd never been the obsessive type, but she'd never been in love before, either, and Elise decided she didn't like it. At all. Love hurt in a way she'd never imagined it could.

The dress she'd worn to the club lay draped across the chair in her new bedroom—the room that used to be her father's—so she picked it up and hung it in the closet, reminding herself why she'd rearranged everything in the first place. A fresh start. That was the goal. As soon as she was well, she intended to sell her father's car and take a trip somewhere far away. If she could get enough for it, she might even enroll in some online classes and work toward getting her degree. If not, she would keep saving, the way she'd planned before Caspian entered her life, and eventually, she'd find her way. She always did.

If her father had taught her nothing else, he'd taught her how to fight her way out of a funk.

Nausea stopped her in the hall, braced with a hand on the wall until the urge to throw up passed, allowing her to continue into the kitchen, where toast and coffee had become the only tolerable breakfast. She ate quickly, already behind, and worried she'd be late for her appointment. Marcus had threatened to cut her hours if she didn't make it to this one—she'd already canceled twice before, and tensions between employer and employee had reached a critical point. It seemed he was taking this second-father role a tad too literally.

But, she reminded herself, it was good that *someone* cared. Though, she sometimes wondered if his concern for her was as much about not wanting to replace her, as it was about her actual well-being.

She showered and dressed, wearing no makeup—which was not unusual—and running out the door with damp hair—which was. When the nurse called her back from the waiting room, Elise gathered her purse and held it to her chest, feeling like a child who was due for boosters or something else traumatic.

The nurse took her weight, her height, her pulse and oxygen levels, and then led her into a sterile room, where Elise was directed to sit on a reclining bed covered in paper and give the nurse her medical history. When asked about her last menstrual cycle, Elise drew a blank. It had been quite a while.

"I'm not sure," she admitted. "But I've had a lot of stress in the last eight months, and haven't been regular for that whole time. I read online that stress can do that."

The nurse paused in her typing to pin Elise with a constructed smile. "It can. I'm sure that's what it is." She made more notes, asked a few more questions, and then directed Elise to the bathroom so she could leave a sample before the doctor came in.

The waiting felt like an eternity, so when he finally arrived, anxiety had twisted her insides into tight little knots, which only loosened slightly when he introduced himself.

"I'm Doctor Meyer." He listened to her breathing through a stethoscope, poked and prodded and asked short, curt questions, and then dragged the stool closer to the examination table. "Elise, how old are you?"

Though she knew it was in her chart, Elise felt compelled to admit, "Nineteen. I'll be twenty in a couple of weeks."

"Would you say that you take good care of yourself? That you're mostly healthy?"

She gulped, afraid to admit that her sleeping and eating habits had gone down the toilet recently. "I try," she said, deciding that it wasn't a lie, because she did try most of the time.

"When was the last time you saw a doctor?"

Again, she had to search the calendar in her brain. "Probably when I was seventeen and had strep."

He pressed his lips together, forming a tight line that cut across his face. "Ideally, you should be seen at least once a year for a well check. I hope you'll change that in the future."

"Yeah, okay." Not sure where his point was going to land, Elise agreed with him simply to move the conversation along so she could get out of here and go home for a nap.

"I'm going to run a full panel of tests on you," he continued. "But I'll tell you now that you have bronchitis, so we're going to go ahead and treat you for that."

Doctor Meyer returned to his computer, tapping away at the keyboard, and leaving Elise wondering what he was writing in her chart. A nurse rapped on the door, then came in and handed the doctor a printed page, which he read, before returning his attention to Elise. "Sweetheart, I don't know how to tell you this, especially because I have a daughter who isn't much younger than you. It's a standard practice to run pregnancy tests before we prescribe medications to young women who are sexually active. Yours came out positive."

The blood drained from her face so quickly that Elise had to lie down to avoid doing a face-plant on the floor. "I'm sorry, what did you say?"

"Of course, we'll run a second test, but these are rarely wrong. Elise, you're pregnant."

Her mouth and throat tasted like someone had attempted to drown her in sawdust, and her shock level rose as rapidly as her heartbeat. "I . . . I can't be. I haven't . . ." But she had, and she knew it. Caspian knew literally nothing about birth control, and she hadn't thought much of it either, though she knew she should have. "Are you sure? Are you really sure?"

Doctor Meyer's face pinched in sympathy. "I understand that you're shocked right now, and I don't blame you. I don't want you to panic, though, because you have options."

Except she didn't. Despite her disbelief over the situation, the one solid thought Elise held onto was that Caspian may have left her, but he'd also given her the gift of family. If she truly was pregnant, she would soon have a child who would love her unconditionally, who would always, always be there, and she couldn't find a bad side to that. Well, other than the financial one. And the physical one. And, well, it was all she could do to take care of herself, let alone another human being. But family.

The doctor continued, "I'm giving you an antibiotic for the bronchitis. It's pregnancy safe, so I don't want you to worry, but it may not work as well as others would. I'll have my nurse draw some blood for those tests, and I want you to schedule another appointment before you leave here. I'd like to get an ultrasound, see if we can get you a timeline as soon as possible." He typed in more orders, then stood. "I understand that this is shocking news for a single woman your age. Take some time to process, and please ask me any questions you can think of, no matter how trivial. Keep a list if necessary. I'm here to help you through this."

Elise met his eyes for perhaps the first time. Chocolate brown, and kind, surrounded by tiny lines that spider-webbed across his temples. "Thank you. I'm okay, at the moment, but I'm sure I'll have lots of questions by tomorrow."

Doctor Meyer tapped her chart on his palm, biting his lip in concern. "You don't seem okay."

Elise blinked, still stunned, but finding that her lips wanted to smile in a way they hadn't when she'd first arrived. "I have bronchitis, and I'm exhausted. And I'm not sure how I can afford a baby, but the news is, surprisingly, not as devastating as I would have expected something like this to be."

"You're in a little bit of shock, I'm afraid. Might take a while to set in, and when it does, I want you to call my office. Doesn't matter what time of night or day—we have a service that always answers and will forward you to my cell if it's an emergency. I'll give them your name. You're going to need someone to talk to."

Elise wiggled off the exam table to follow the doctor out of the room. "Thank you," she said, still reeling and, as he'd warned, in a large degree of shock. "I'm still okay to work, right?"

He nodded, handing her a sample bottle of vitamins. "For now. We'll see as things progress, but if you don't have insurance, I suggest you get to filling out paperwork for financial assistance right away. No matter what you decide, or how this goes, you're going to need medical care, and we don't want that to add to your burdens." They passed the nurse's station and he retrieved two printed pages. "I want you back here before the end of the week."

She hadn't seen a doctor in so long that Elise half expected a lollipop and balloon as exit prizes for being good—instead she walked away with an invoice, telling her how much she owed for the visit, a prescription for drugs she felt hesitant to take, and an appointment to come back in two days.

Sometimes it sucked to be a grownup.

Chapter Nineteen

AFTER RUSSELL LEFT—STILL HAVING never admitted to their mother that he'd come home for a surprise visit—Caspian had no one to advise him on what to wear or what to say or how best to approach Elise at the Turtle, but he knew that a conversation was necessary.

Elise hurt, and so did he, and it was time to make things right, as Russell had advised.

That afternoon, his mother returned to her work as a nurse, explaining to Caspian that she'd been called to cover a shift at the hospital. She had taken as much time off as she dared, but she'd return tomorrow to get started on their bucket list of experiences.

So many holes in his heart had been filled now that he'd found his mother and brother. And Elise. She, alone, had become a central focus of his every need, and with each hour that passed when he wasn't with her, that need became clearer than the water in which he used to live.

Sitting on the bed in his room, Caspian fidgeted with the large, clear stone his mother had given him, holding it up to the light and watching as it refracted rainbows across the walls and ceiling and floor. His father did have a thing for sparkly, human baubles—so obsessed, that he had outlawed them in Atlantis, and then confiscated all that any of the Mer had collected—be they found items from shipwrecks, or stolen from humans who were stupid enough to bring such items too close to the water. And though the Sea King had attempted to be secretive about where these items were stored, Caspian knew. He'd lived in the palace since he was six, and done more than his share of exploring. His father had an entire cave filled with gold and silver and gems of every size and color. Were the cave ever to be discovered by humans, even the richest of pirates would be shocked by such a discovery.

But this cave was connected to the dungeons in Atlantis, which made human access impossible. As a leader, his father was fair, and for the most part, kind—but even *he* had his strange obsession, his flaw. Caspian knew, now, that must devise a way to exploit that weakness. Perhaps he would offer to purchase the creature that Maui had brought to Atlantis, as it was the origin of the poison Caspian needed to continue his life ashore.

He closed the stone in his fist and stood, staring into a closet full of clothes he wasn't sure how to match. He could not return to Atlantis without first speaking to Elise. He'd promised, and whether she remained angry or not, Caspian could not fail to keep promises made to his beloved. Others perhaps, but not her. Not ever. Once he'd showered and dressed, he stared in the mirror at his pendant. A bright, purple pearl had loosened from the rest of the strand, begging to be removed, so Caspian pulled it off. He tugged a leather lace from a child-sized shoe in Russell's closet, and drew it through the hole in the tiny bead. This would be his gift to Elise—his promise to return.

Walking the five miles to the Turtle was no big deal to Caspian, especially as he was able to stop along the way and pick flowers, which he knew would soften her anger, if even a little. The cool breeze coming off the water served as a constant reminder that Caspian must journey home—that he would need to swim sooner than later. It also reminded him of the days—and nights—he'd spent with the woman he longed to keep. Staying here would be worth whatever sacrifices he must make in Atlantis. Being with her was worth *more* than his kingdom.

He entered The Sea Turtle through the front, and claimed his usual booth. Minutes later, Elise pushed through the swinging door, reminding Caspian of his first breath of air upon reaching land. She carried a tray loaded with meals, and strode directly to the table where the food was to be delivered, but when her eyes landed on Caspian, her step faltered, and the tray wobbled precariously. Caspian jumped up to help, but before he could get there, Elise had re-gained control of the tray and re-painted the smile on her face as she set each entrée in front of the customers.

When she'd finished, she took a straight path to Caspian. "What are you doing here?"

She seemed such a mix of emotions, Caspian couldn't tell if she was angry, or hurt, or annoyed, or . . . something else entirely. It didn't help his confidence. "I've come to see you." He picked up the flowers he'd lain on the table, offering them to Elise.

The lines on her face softened, but tears welled in her eyes. "You're leaving, aren't you?"

"Not for long," he promised. "I must take care of a matter, but I intend to return. For good. Forever."

She tilted her head, drawing a finger over the scars where his gills had sealed closed. "We both know that's not possible. You'll die if you stay here too long."

He covered her hand on his neck with his. "Perhaps not. There is one possibility, but I must return home to receive it."

Her eyes filled. "Don't. Please don't make promises you can't keep."

196

Seeing that they'd drawn the attention of other diners, Caspian steered Elise toward the back room where they would have less of an audience, but Elise pulled him out the back door instead, which was even better.

"Beloved, I have never promised something I could not give, something I could not do. I have been very careful about that since I first arrived."

She swallowed. "I know, and I don't want you to start now. I need, more than ever, for our memories to be sweet and happy. I don't ever want to resent you or regret our time together. I can't. Even if I would have, it's too late, now."

Something in her eyes, her watery smile, the conviction behind her words, set off an alarm in Caspian. "Elise, what is it? I feel that there is something more I should know."

Her face lit up as tears rolled down her cheeks. "I wasn't going to tell you. It won't change anything, and might make it harder for you to leave. I don't want that. I couldn't live with having you die, just because you feel a responsibility to me."

He took her in his arms, and she wrapped hers around him so tightly that Caspian knew something grave weighed on her—something more than his impending departure. "Elise, I intend to return with the one thing that might keep me breathing here. It will cost everything I have in Atlantis—and be well worth the price."

She pulled back, her face wet, and rubbed it against the front of his shirt—which didn't bother Caspian in the least. "You would do that?"

"I intend to do it," he corrected. "For you. And my mother and brother. I have never had a true family before, and now that I understand what it is like, I cannot give it up, or let it go."

She pulled away completely, lacing her fingers into her hair and pulling tight as if to clarify her thoughts. "You want to stay—for family? Are you sure?"

"Beloved, I would not say such things if I did not mean them. I will not lie, and offer promises that my strategy will go as planned. So many things could keep me from it. What I can promise is that I will return to you, or be willing to die in the attempt."

Her arms dropped to her sides, both hands immediately covering her stomach. "I'm going to tell you something, and I don't want you to freak out, okay? I'm not saying it to scare you away or make you feel obligated to me or—anyone. I just—if you're leaving, and whatever you're going to do is dangerous, I want you to know, just—because you deserve to."

His hands rested on her shoulders, half afraid she might collapse, from the exhaustion of her illness. "You may tell me anything. I will not—freak out, as you say— though I am not sure what that means."

She brushed her palm over his shoulder, cupped his jaw in her hand. "Caspian, I'm pregnant. Went to the doctor for my bronchitis the other day, and they did two tests—both came back positive. Guess I should have been more prepared, smarter—I don't know. But I'm not upset over it, and I'm not sorry. I want this child, even if you can never come back, because having him or her in my life will be like having a piece of you, forever. So, if something happens and you can't get back to me—just know that I'm going to be okay, and so is our child."

A cyclone of emotions swirled in his heart and brain and all through his blood. Shock, disbelief, joy, anger, despair, elation, happiness, longing. He was going to be a father? With Elise? He hadn't known for certain that such a thing was possible between human and Mer—though his being half-human himself should have provided a hint.

He dropped his hands from her, at a loss for the best way to react, and devastated that he'd caused her such heartache. "I have dishonored you."

"No. No, you haven't." She shook her head, adamant. "You have *loved* me, and this is the result. I'm *honored* to carry this child. We may not be bound by law, but in the most spiritual sense, we have been as one, and that's enough."

Caspian shook his head, emotions he'd rarely felt bursting from his facial orifices. "It is not enough, Elise.

I shall go to Atlantis and do what is necessary, and then I will return to you and our youngling." He withdrew the pearl he'd strung onto the leather, and opened the strand to slip it over her head, where it hung against her chest, just below her throat. "This is my promise to you—I will return, and if you find such a proposition favorable, we will be joined for eternity."

Her lips quirked, but she couldn't quite smile, and her hand protected the pearl as if it were a priceless treasure. "Let's work on one thing at a time. First, you get back to me, and if you do—when you do—I'd like to talk, in private, at my house. Then we'll see what we see, okay?"

Caspian nodded. "Yes. I will return, my love, and I will find you."

Elise held the bouquet of flowers to her nose. "Please hurry. We have just under eight months before this little one arrives—I'd love for you to be here when he or she comes."

He kissed her then, drawing her into his arms as if having their bodies touch through clothes would never be enough—because it wouldn't. This family that he'd found in Oceanside continued to grow, stretching his heart into something other—something bigger and more meaningful and real. Nothing and no one in Atlantis mattered to him so much as Elise and his child—and he would do whatever it took to return to them.

Chapter Twenty

ELISE WATCHED CASPIAN LEAVE. HE was heading home to his mother, a woman Elise had still not met. She knew he needed to tie up loose ends before returning to Atlantis, but it was hard to come second to another woman and not resent it—at least a little bit. And though this woman was obviously not a romantic threat, she was still the reason Caspian had left Elise in the first place, and the reason she hadn't heard from him since—until last night.

Waiting tables helped to distract her thoughts, and she focused every ounce of her energy on doing her job well. She made record time between orders and delivery, smiled and laughed and filled her pockets with tips, all the while, reminding herself that Caspian came from a different culture, that he had never dated, never learned the expectations of human women.

Knowing so didn't help much. Nothing could change the fact that love and expectation were entirely separate things—and Elise had undeniably connected the two in an unhealthy way.

"Excuse me, Miss? I think you gave us someone else's order." An older gentleman, dressed in a business suit, sat at the corner table with a woman who must be half his age, and who'd dressed far more casually in shorts and a tank top. They both had hair the same shade of auburn, and golden-hazel eyes, so Elise deducted that the woman must be his daughter.

She hurried to the table, glancing at the entrees remaining on her platter and shaking her head— Marcus was getting sick of having to make these things a second time, and though he'd been patient with her, she knew that patience was wearing thin. "I'm so sorry, sir." She placed the correct entrée in front of him, her eyes flickering to the young lady's food. "Is yours all right?" The lady nodded as Elise went to take back the unwanted burger—and then left it. "I can't serve this to anyone else, so would either of you like to have it? On the house, of course."

When neither wanted it, Elise picked it up and took it back to the kitchen, where she planned to package it in a to-go bag and set aside—for what, she wasn't sure. Sighing, she shoved through the swinging door. "Marcus, I did it again. I'm going to need another deluxe with sweet potato fries. I'm so sorry." She set

202

down the platter as a wave of dizziness washed over her, and braced her hands on the counter while she waited for it to pass.

Marcus sent a new entrée through the window to Shelley and asked her to deliver it to the right person, then approached Elise from behind. "How far along are you?"

Elise whirled, cursing herself for it, when her head continued to spin long after her body stopped moving. "What?"

Marcus took her by the shoulders and directed her to a stool. "You heard me. I know you had an appointment at the clinic, because I got the bill—but you've never said anything about results, and while your cough sounds better, it's obvious there's more. I'm not stupid, Elise. I've known enough pregnant women to see the signs. You tire easily, you turn green at certain smells, you get dizzy after being on your feet for a few hours, you're emotional, and you've traded away all your morning shifts. Now, I'm sorry if you don't want to talk about it, but at least give me something to work with so I know how to schedule you, and can pay attention to times when I might need to call in backup."

As if Marcus had flipped a switch, tears sprung into Elise's eyes, falling before she even recognized that they were there. "I'm not sure. I have another appointment tomorrow. Doctor Meyer's going to do an ultrasound and figure it out, but I'm guessing I'll be due sometime late spring, or early summer."

Marcus handed her a paper towel to wipe her eyes, then stepped away to fill a glass with water, which he also offered to Elise. "Only a few weeks along, then."

Elise accepted the water and gulped, feeling a stab to the heart as she acknowledged how much her life had changed since Caspian had walked into it. "Most likely. To be honest, Marcus, I'm not sure. All I know is that I'll do everything I can to be a good mother. Can't think much past that right now."

He dragged a stool to sit in front of her, glimpsing over the pass-through, to make sure no new orders waited. "Does Caspian know?"

More tears, more wiping, and a few sobs ripped from her throat. "He does now. I wasn't going to tell him, but he came to say goodbye before he went home, and I just . . . it just came out."

Marcus straightened, fury firing in his eyes. "He knows, and he left anyway? Are you serious?"

Elise pulled in a calming breath, willing her emotions to settle. "He didn't have a choice. We both knew he was only here temporarily."

"Is he coming back?"

She swallowed, and luckily, some of her shaky emotions went down too. "I don't know. He says he is, that he wants to, and I think he has every intention of coming back. The question is when."

Marcus swore, using words he never used in front of his employees. "Exactly why he never should have left in the first place. Real men do not desert their own children and leave girlfriends as single mothers. Only cowards run away scared. You're better off without him anyway." He stood, rubbing a hand over Elise's shoulder. "I got your back, honey. You and that kid are going to be fine."

Shelley stuck another order page on the turn wheel, so Marcus walked away to retrieve it, leaving Elise alone to finish her water and catch her breath. She had no doubt that her job here was secure—that as long as she could work, she'd have the necessary money to get by. But now that she was responsible for another person, getting by wasn't enough anymore.

"This is going to be cold on your tummy." The nurse covered Elise's stomach in clear gel, then pressed the smooth device to her skin, continually moving it around as she studied the blurs of black and white and gray on the monitor near Elise's head. A steady rhythm emitted from the speakers, a sound that made Elise's throat clog with joy.

"How do you know what all of it is?" She asked, trying to make sense of the seemingly shapeless blobs.

"It was hard when I first started. But I get better with each one." The nurse's face lit up and a smile bloomed as she pressed her finger to a tiny, moving line. "There we go. Right here. See that movement? That's the heartbeat." She used the machine to snap a screen shot, then moved it again and took three more before removing the device and handing Elise a towel to wipe off the gel. While Elise cleaned up, the nurse marked each picture with a series of X's and measurements. When she was finished, she stood, squinting at the printed page as the machine spit it out. "We're going to call this due date June 21st, which puts you at four or five weeks. But I feel like that's got to be wrong, because these measurements seem really small compared to your symptoms. Doctor Meyer will be in soon, and I'm sure he'll have a better explanation."

Before she stepped out, the nurse raised the head of the examination table, allowing Elise to lie back, while remaining partially upright. When the doctor entered, he wore a frown that set Elise's nerves on edge. "I'm glad you came back," he said, pulling the stool from where the nurse had left it so he could face Elise. "An ultrasound is one of those fail-proof pregnancy tests that more women should have in the beginning, in my opinion. Gives us better guidelines as to what each pregnancy and each new mother might require." He held up Elise's chart, with the pictures attached. "You're measuring really small, and that makes it hard for us to get a definite due date. On the other hand, the fact that we got decent ultrasound shots this early is beyond incredible. Even with the best technology out there, an external ultrasound wouldn't usually pick up a fetus this tiny."

"What does that mean?" Anxiety piled onto Elise with each word, each glance between doctor and nurse.

Doctor Meyer pressed his lips together while he studied the photos again. "I'm not sure." He flipped through her chart to look at other pages. "You're naturally a small person, so I don't want you to be concerned about the size yet, as the cause could be genetics, but your blood tests have some abnormalities that concern me."

"What kind of abnormalities?"

The nurse leaned over his shoulder, squinting at the page. "I've never seen that before."

"Me either." Doctor Meyer shook his head and let the pages fall back into place. "Let's not stress about it now. It's early in your pregnancy. An abnormal test can be caused by anything from the anti-biotics you're taking, to something you ate that was hormonally treated—anything you've done that might throw your body off. We'll give you a few weeks and run the test again, just to be sure."

Elise let out a relieved sigh. "So, I don't need to worry about my baby?"

Doctor Meyer shared a surreptitious glance with the nurse. "Not yet. But I do want you to keep in the back of your mind that there's a slight possibility that you could miscarry, or that your child could be born with some type of birth defect." He paused to let that sink in, while Elise fought more tears. She'd become leakier than a sinking ship. "As I said, I want to run more tests," he continued. "And see you back in two weeks to discuss the results."

As the doctor left the room, Elise accepted a throw up bucket from the nurse, who'd seen her struggle and was prepared. It was the first time her whole pregnancy that Elise had actually thrown up.

Chapter Twenty-One

CASPIAN HAD TURNED A RECLINER toward the window to give him a view of the road, and sat waiting, tapping his fingers on the velvet arm with impatience. Mother was going to be disappointed, perhaps even angry, but this could not be helped. Not now.

He hadn't planned to go back so soon, but after talking to Elise and finding out that he was going to be a father, the necessary trip felt more immediately pressing—especially with Elise worried about him losing time while he was below. In truth, if his mother hadn't given him a birthdate and presented factual evidence of how long he'd been gone, he would never have believed it. He knew he'd grown a lot since leaving Oceanside, and that quite a bit of time had passed, but the Mer didn't keep track of years in the same way as humans. Everything to them centered around the changing of tides, moon cycles, and the temperature variations in the water—which wasn't much in their portion of the deep, wide sea.

Here on land, time was kept according to the cycles of the sun and rotation of the earth. From the timeline Elise had mentioned, Caspian felt confident that both human and Mer females carried their young for about the same length of time—which wasn't long at all, for a man returning to a city below the sea, and desperate to return before the birth of his child.

As much as he'd convinced himself that Maui maintained a stash of the precious poison, or that his father would allow him to take the creature that made it, a vein of doubt remained, and through that vein, his blood thickened and pulsed while he waited for his mother to return from her job. If Caspian was somehow unable to return, he wanted his mother to know his child, to know Elise. He had to make sure they were taken care of.

A car passed by, but it wasn't his mother's. Then another, and another, and soon he'd lost count, his fingers digging into the upholstery until he'd poked a tiny hole in the underside of the arm. He'd learned about clocks and how they worked, when he'd taken his job at the resort, but hadn't yet learned how to gauge the time that passed during his mother's shift. When the sun dipped below the sea on the far-off horizon, he stood, too anxious to wait any longer.

He found a notebook and pen, and carefully drew what might pass for letters, which he hoped turned into words that his mother could understand. He wrote:

Dear Mother,

I am sorry to leave so soon. I must return to Atlantis to secure a way for me to remain ashore permanently. I shall go out to sea the same way I came, by way of the private cove I showed you on that first day. If I am unable to return, please look after my Elise. She is family now, as I intend to make her my wife upon my earliest opportunity. You will find her at The Sea Turtle.

Thank you for giving me life, and renewing my purpose.

Your Caspian.

He set the note in the center of the kitchen table, along with the jewels he'd gathered for Elise. This was all he had to give, and he hoped it was enough. He retrieved the diamond from the dresser in his room—Russell's room—and slid on his shoes, hoping he could find his way back to the cove on foot. As he stepped onto the porch, a gust of wind blew the door shut, and unbeknownst to Caspian, blew his note off the table and under the refrigerator.

Sea so Blue

As he rounded the corner at the end of the block, he turned back for one last memory, praying that he would someday see this view again.

Cool, sparkling water flowed over the scales that had re-appeared seconds after his submersion in the sea. Afraid of offending his father, Caspian left his clothes and human trimmings—along with his pendant—in the cove, bringing with him only the diamond his mother had given him. It seemed such a small thing, this tiny, sparkling rock, and yet somehow he understood—as his mother had—the nature of his father's obsession. He'd amassed a gigantic, vast collection, even though the baubles served no other purpose than to look pretty.

This stone remained his strongest hope, and absolute last resort. He could not offer it to his father until all other attempts were lost—as Caspian suspected would happen. His father had a strong will. But Caspian's own will, and his newfound determination, was infinitely stronger. Giving up a kingdom and a throne seemed such small things compared to what he stood to lose in Oceanside.

He hastened to the arch that marked the location, and then allowed current to draw him down, down, and down again, through the tunnels that would expel him at the gates of Atlantis. The temperatures dropped, and pressure built, until his human lungs contracted and his head throbbed, chest tightening with each inch that he descended.

Memories of his too-short childhood filled his head—grief, terror, utter confusion—and the anger that burned inside him flourished, its flame reaching toward his father like a dry, dead plant—hot, bright and unstoppable.

By the time he arrived at the guarded gate, bravery and fury warred inside him. He ignored the guard's demand to halt and swam into the city. The sentry pursued him, shouting threats of torture, captivity, and worse, and finally, Caspian stopped, anger shooting from his eyes, and electricity tingling in his hands. "How dare you demand things of your Prince. I am Caspian, son of Tangaroa, Prince of Atlantis and heir to the throne. I have returned from my travels ashore."

The guard straightened, strands of yellow, purple, and green hair floating around his face, neck, and shoulders. He snapped his fin and fisted his hand, crossing his arm over his heart—the customary salute to Mer royalty. "I apologize, my Prince. Please forgive my mistake—your skin has browned, and your shorn hair lightened as if a sea witch has laid upon you a vile curse."

To this, Caspian laughed, wondering what the merman would think of the fiery-haired, smooth-skinned Elise, whose soft, sweet voice could not even be compared to that of a Mer female. Certainly, a merman without human lungs should have reason to fear her a witch. She had enthralled him entirely, and convinced him to give up his life and become part of her world. "I have been ashore, and ashore is where I shall soon return." Annoyed with the distraction, Caspian started for the palace, leaving the guard behind, stunned.

The swim paths of Atlantis leapt with activity. Similar to human-style roads, each path cut past living quarters and places of business, lined with colorful corals and ridges and bright seashells to mark each location. In the market, customers purchased and traded for shells, food, interesting salvage pieces, and exotic types of paihana, while others offered fish or kelp, and all manner of delicacies. Some merchants packed their goods for the end of the business day, because the change of tide grew near.

Caspian washed through town in haste, noting how many eyes focused on his face, his shorn hair, his lack of the markings or other coverings typical to the Atlantian Mer, and then he noted how they followed his path as if drawn toward the radiant blue light that kept the city aglow.

If he were to remain here, this would be his fate forever—always watched, always noticed, never free from scrutiny.

In the distance, the palace rose, jagged edges spearing toward the upper sea, magnificent in size, and intimidating, as the mother-of-pearl iridescent walls glimmered with every movement of the tide. When he reached the pearl and seashell encrusted door, it did not automatically open as he expected, so he pounded on it. "I am Caspian, son of Tangaroa, and I demand that you admit me into my home."

The door swung open, and a huffing, snail of a merman appeared on the other side, his face pink with anxiety. "I am sorry, my Prince. I did not—"

"I know. You did not recognize me." Caspian brushed by the servant and continued to his father's receiving room, where the Sea King would be found hearing the complaints of city-dwelling Mer. "Father," he boomed. "I have returned, and I must speak with you at once." But while a smattering of servants remained in the gathering space, the Sea King did not.

Caspian whirled on the snail-like servant who had ushered him in, annoyed to find the merman so close that they nearly collided. "Back off if you do not wish me to flatten you," he said, not realizing that he'd picked up some very human expressions.

More apologies and bumbling explanations, which Caspian shut down with one finger. "Where is my father? I must speak with him immediately."

The servant straightened. "The Sea King has gone hunting, but is due to return with the change of the waking tide."

Caspian blinked, frustrated and annoyed at the timing, because he did not feel at all capable of waiting through the night to explain his drastic choices. "What about my cousin Maui?"

"Sir," the servant said, wringing his hands. "Maui has gone ashore and has not yet returned."

This brought Caspian up short. "Gone ashore? When?"

"Shortly after you left," the servant replied. "Your father does not expect his return within our city."

"Never?"

"I believe not, my Prince."

The news hit Caspian like a ray-stinger to the abdomen. Of all the worst-case scenarios he had imagined, this was not on the list. His exhausted muscles tensed, and though his pulse had slowed with the temperature drop between shore and sea, the steady thrum pulsed in his temples, drumming at his concentration. He lifted his head in the way his father had taught him, aligned with his straightened spine, and swished past the servant. "Very well. I shall return to my chambers, where I demand a meal, and to have my bed prepared. Then dismiss all guards and servants from my space until the waking tide."

The servant saluted in the same way the guard had, with an arm over his chest, hand fisted, while he swished his tail. "Yes, my Prince. It shall be done, sir."

Caspian took to his chambers, determined to come up with a new plan of action. He would not allow an absent father and missing cousin to keep him from Elise and his child. He would simply have to find another way.

Once the servants had left him to sleep, he sneaked out of his room, resolved to find the sea creature from whom the poison had been harvested. His father kept it somewhere secret, but Caspian had experience with roaming the most secret spaces in the palace, and that is where he began. First, the treasure cave, which Caspian felt certain that no other Mer—servants included—knew existed. A large, dark space, littered with years and years of secret collecting, sparkling gems, gleaming gold and tarnished silver, even green-coated copper. Coins and jewels and statues and drinkware— all manner of human luxuries, but not a single living thing, aside from the tiny plankton always present in the water.

Next, he searched his father's chamber. This space remained one of the few secured by an actual door—knotted wood, coated in mother of pearl, and created to match the grand palace entry. Each movement of water sent ripples of color bouncing off the surface, sapphire and lavender, rose, peach and silver, a literal rainbow of subdued sparkle. Such a door screamed of excess, even in the underwater city, even as protection for the Sea King's private space.

Before his visit to shore, Caspian had not paid much attention to such details. But time spent with Elise, who worked long and hard to remain in her home and to fill her cabinets with food, left him acutely aware of the value of *things*. Even the waterways through the city, lined with shells and pearls and other shiny, glistening markers, boasted of a rich economy and lack of the awareness that Caspian had so recently gained.

The problem was not that the Mer took such things for granted, so much as that humans put extreme value on them, while the Mer did not. Humans lived and died according to what they owned or could purchase, while the Mer simply survived day-to-day, and occasionally enjoyed an unusual treat, such as paihana.

He crept inside his father's chamber and closed the lovely door behind him. Significantly larger than Caspian's, the space had been appointed with the finest quality of hammock-bed, thick floorings of woven sea-grass and kelp that covered an intricate mosaic stone design, held together by hardened clay. The walls, too, had been embedded with lovely patterns and intricate seascapes, and each wall curved into the next, creating an oblong pattern that ended in the same place where it began.

Perhaps the Mer did not put value on *things*, so much as on beauty. Atlantis had its imperfections as well.

Cut into the thick, stone walls, and designed as part of the mosaic, Caspian found all manner and size of shelves, on which had been placed containers of every scope and variety, stone tablets, a collection of coronets, neck adornments, and armored cuffs made for both upper and lower arms. Gold-plated chest armor sat propped inside a large niche that had been carved into the stone, and a glowing gold trident lay next to it. All memories of wars long past, wars Caspian hoped must never be fought again. He inspected each item, tested the contents of the vessels and containers, and finally fell into his father's hammock bed, exhausted and confused.

He dragged his foot along the ground, trying to decide where he should explore next. His toe caught on the rug, shifting it out of place. He bent to straighten it, and noticed a corner of wood peeking out on the far side of the circular room. Caspian peeled back the heavy seagrass to find a thick, wooden door built into the floor. *This*, he thought. *This is what I've been looking for. Secrets. All the secrets of Atlantis.*

Opening the hatch proved difficult, so Caspian heaved with all his strength, and once his fingers could fit between door and frame, the suction of water helped do the rest, slamming the hinged-hatch open to a dark, narrow corridor that appeared endless in its inky, black expanse.

He stuck his head into the space, hoping that his vision would adjust, but the darkness remained, covering whatever lay beyond in a blanket of secrecy. "Light," he muttered. "I need light." Once again, he inspected the shelves in his father's room, finding a pail of Paihana—the newly discovered mind-altering recreational drink, invented by Maui—from which he inhaled a long sip—an extra dose of courage. When he found none of the glowing plankton that were used to light the city, Caspian worried that he'd have to leave the King's personal cavern and journey to the servants' section of spaces, where plankton and other such things were stored. Frustrated, he stared at the open hatch, unwilling to close it again, but also unwilling to leave this space without answers.

He ran his fingers over the armor, and then his father's tall, gold and seashell coronet, wishing himself braver, better equipped for such exploration. When the crown lit with a pale green glow, he stopped, staring. This particular circlet was one his father had worn many times throughout Caspian's time with him, but he had never seen it glow. More curious than ever, Caspian ran his fingers over the trident, feeling a buzz of power zing up his arm from the lightest touch. The Sea King's tools could not be used by another Mer, until the next Sea King claimed the throne—that Mer being born royal.

Perhaps Caspian, being in line to inherit this crown, had begun to come into his power. He gulped another swig of Paihana and lifted the coronet to his head, enjoying the extra weight atop his short hair as he picked up the trident, and pointed it at the dark corridor, grinning when a shaft of light cut through the dark.

"That will do." He dove into the shadowy space, seeking answers to all the questions that plagued him—specifically, how he was going to return to his family on land.

Chapter Twenty-Two

CASPIAN MADE HIS WAY THROUGH the black tunnel, made only marginally brighter by the light of the trident. The confined space squeezed in on him from all sides, and the murky water carried a distinct scent that bespoke of brackish filth. The tunnel opened into a small room, where it dead-ended. Caspian turned one way, and then the next, observing cages, nets, and corrals, each holding captive creature upon creature, from turtles crowded inside small cages, to dolphins chained to the icy, stone wall. Octopus, squid, eels, snakes, and even a clear jar, made of ice, containing hundreds of tiny seahorses.

"Father," he murmured. "How could you? This cruelty is madness personified." He proceeded to the cage nearest him and unhooked the latch, preparing to free them all, before his father could return—but then he considered his objective. The poison. How was he to know which creature was the one he needed? What if each of these creatures served a purpose?

Though incensed by the inhumane conditions in which the creatures were kept, Caspian could not yet free them. Not before learning which one he'd come to find. He returned to his father's cavern empty-handed, and replaced first the hatch, and then the rug, vowing to return and free every last creature. He replaced the circlet and the trident on the shelf, and checked to be sure he hadn't disturbed anything else.

Next up: Maui's room.

Though he had been gone for quite some time, Caspian had spent his youth exploring the corridors, including all the most hidden spaces. Or, most of them, at least. The one in his father's room was not something he'd discovered before, and he was certain others must exist—but Caspian was no longer a child seeking a place to hide from his life. This time, he sought a treasure, much like the pirates he'd dreamed of each night as he lay in his hammock bed and tried so valiantly to remember the stories his mother had told him.

Maui, also of royal blood, had been given the cavern nearest to Caspian's own, for while Caspian stood to inherit the rule of Atlantis, Maui stood to inherit Oceania, another city of Mer. With only minimal lighting from the sleep-time plankton, Caspian made his way to the empty room, shoving past the privacy curtain, woven of seagrass and kelp, to study what little his cousin had left behind.

The empty hammock swung lightly in the movement that followed Caspian, a loose strand brushing across the silt floor, stirring a cloud around Caspian's re-forming fin. On a stone table, he discovered a pair of shiny wrist cuffs, and several delicate, and not-so-delicate, neck adornments. Some thick with shells and stones and wildly colorful corals, and others slim, bedecked with pearls and grasses and shiny threads of silver and gold.

Caspian lifted each one, inspecting them. Might any have been soaked in the poison? When none elicited an urge for him to breathe through his lungs, rather than gills, he decided that these adornments would be of no use, and moved on.

A nearby ledge held a giant clamshell filled with bright purple gel-thick liquid, which he immediately recognized as the Paihana Maui had brought with him from Oceania. Next to the large shell sat a palm-sized, empty one, and Caspian used it to scoop out a slurp of the Paihana, pressing it to his lips for an experimental sip.

Unlike the pleasant, sweet Paihana to which Caspian had grown accustomed, Maui's favored concoction had a bitter tang that sent a burning, numbing sensation across his tongue before he even took it into his mouth. Shuddering with disgust, he closed the lid on the smaller clam and stowed it in the pouch next to the diamond.

A small alcove held a stack of thin clay sheets, on which words had been carved. The Mer equivalent of a book. Caspian lifted the first, skimming over the etchings, and finding only a basic accounting of Maui's thoughts from a particularly rough day. The next one became of more interest, when it brought up Maui's suspicion that the Sea King of Atlantis maintained a trove of illegal human treasure—though Maui could think of no reason why there should be a need for such items.

Four tablets later, Caspian found himself engrossed in a tale of royal intrigue, starring his father, cousin Maui, and . . . then himself. Maui wrote:

Though the Sea King denies such a claim, it has become clear that my half-human cousin might be the only subject on which I might successfully test the venom-soaked pearls.

The merman, Cannon, did not survive our risky experiment, though he walked the shore for moments, long enough to fulfill his dying wish. In attempt to achieve my goal, I have run out of Mer who are willing to overlook the risks. I must make my last effort on the only remaining possibility: a merman who is also half human, and therefore hatched with fully-formed human lungs, which need only to re-inflate.

Caspian paused, rereading the passage again. He'd been part of an experiment? This was not something of which he'd been aware. He'd gone ashore hoping to find his mother, and perhaps to come to know his human side, while postponing his union with Marietta—but no one had explained anything about deadly risks.

He set down that page and picked up the next.

The young Prince is betrothed to join with a mermaid for which he has not yet gained affection. I do not expect much resistance once I present the possibility that he might pay a visit to his family ashore.

I have harvested the remaining poison from the octopus, and must now surrender her to the Sea King, as I have surrendered my other experimental creatures. 1,460 more tides must pass before the blue rings reappear and the octopus produces the correct potency of venom for another attempt.

Horrified, Caspian realized that the animals his father had hidden must not be his own, but Maui's. Still, he wondered why they remained captive. Then he wondered how his father had allowed him, Caspian, to become a subject for one of Maui's experiments. What if his lungs had no longer worked? Would he, too, have suffocated?

He lifted the next tablet, disgust and confusion warring in his muscles, leaving his shoulders tense, forearms tight from gripping the page, and his fin stilled, leaving him hovering just above the silt ground. Maui's writing continued on one last tablet.

The Sea King has agreed to my terms, and the Prince is eager to visit shore. I must now leave Atlantis and watch from afar, for if the Prince shall perish, then I shall be sentenced to death.

I can take nothing with me and risk the suspicion of Atlantian guards, thus I have tasked a trusted partner and ally, Tuck, with guarding the remaining venom. Should the experiment succeed, all future royals will have access to a means of escape, should they wish, as every royal is born a half-breed. They need only to locate Tuck.

Caspian's heart thrummed in his chest. He'd been mistaken in believing that the venom would be found within the walls of the palace, and he did not know a merman called Tuck. Atlantis had grown into a thriving city of countless Mer. Finding the keeper of the venom would not be an easy task, but Caspian considered Elise, his mother, Russell, and his growing child, and a sense of urgency drove him to try.

Ignoring the remaining adornments, Caspian stacked the tablets together and hauled them to his room, where he concealed them in his wardrobe, beneath the possessions he had accumulated over years spent in the palace. Though the urge to continue the search pressed him forward, he resisted, recognizing the shift in the current that indicated another change of tide. His father would return at any moment, but Caspian could not leave Atlantis without the venom. He must find Tuck, even if it required playing the part of the Prince returned home.

Seething with frustration, he flopped into his hammock, begging his mind and body to rest. He would need his energy for battling in the coming tides.

Caspian woke to the shrill, nasal voice of his father's aide, Glan. "I present King, Tangaroa, ruler of Atlantis, son of Earth and Sky, Brother to Tangaloa, ruler of Oceania, and father to Caspian, heir to the Atlantian throne." The earsplitting voice grated on his nerves, which, Caspian suspected, was the reason Glan had been invited to accompany the Sea King for a visit to his son's private cavern.

His father entered, and Caspian forced his heavy eyes to open, blinking to focus, and wondering if the older merman's shoulders had always been so wide, his muscles so corded and thick. Gray hair had woven between the rainbow locks that cascaded around

Tangaroa's head and shoulders, and down his back, and wrinkles marred his smooth, golden skin in places where they hadn't when Caspian had first faced his father.

"Hello, my son. I've come to welcome you home, at last."

The Anger that had festered in Caspian bubbled, hot and strong, but Caspian knew he must play a part until he could track down Tuck. He pasted on a respectful smile, and rose to greet his father with the traditional Atlantian salute. "Hello father. I have returned to Atlantis, as you desired."

Ignoring the salute, Tangaroa embraced his son— something he hadn't done since Caspian's first day in the palace. "I warned you that land-living was no place for a Mer Prince. Such unrest, turmoil. Humans cannot be trusted."

Confusion melded with Caspian's suspicion, spinning his instincts into a whirlwind of perplexity. His experience had been very much the opposite of his father's words, first with Elise and the people at the Turtle, followed by his friends at the resort, and then with his mother and Russell. But Caspian refused to share such details, opting instead to take the conversation in a different direction. "I should still like to postpone my joining." His new life, new friends, had changed him irrevocably, and in these short moments, he realized that he no longer feared his father.

Tangaroa regarded Glan, who inspected a tablet he'd been holding against his bare chest. "Thirty tides before the next full moon."

"Very well." Tangaroa dismissed Glan with a wave of his hand, returning his attention to Caspian. "I will allow you thirty tides. On the thirty-first, when moonlight pierces the deepest blue to kiss the sands of Atlantis, you will join with Marietta, your betrothed."

Caspian's stomach twisted with revulsion, but he willed himself to agree. It would do no good for him to argue now. "Thank you, Father. For allowing me time, and also for giving me leave to journey ashore in search of my mother."

The wrinkles in his father's face deepened with sorrow. "And did you? Find her?"

"I did. She continues to live in the home where we resided during my childhood."

"How is she?" Fondness leaked through the Sea King's voice in a way Caspian had never heard his father speak—to, or about, anyone.

"She is wonderful." Caspian made a conscious effort to control his body and avoid giving away his own feelings. "She has a new family, a new son. She welcomed me into her home, as a mother should, but I am different now, as is she, and land life proved more difficult than I envisioned." The lie tasted bitter on his tongue, but he could see no way around it.

"I am glad to know that Mona lives, and thrives, in her new life. She provided Atlantis with an heir, and for that I will forever hold her in my highest esteem."

Silence fell between them. Caspian fought every urge to question his father about Mona, and about his own descent to Atlantis. Instead, he flopped into his hammock, exaggerating his exhaustion. "Father, I have, only moments ago, retired to rest, and my return journey from land has worn down my energy. I should like to rest now, that I might be refreshed and join you for last meal, to regale you with tales of my adventures ashore."

Tangaroa drifted through the privacy curtain, his mind already far away. "Very well. You shall rest, my son. But do not forget that Marietta longs to be greeted by her betrothed. Do not torture her further."

Yawning, Caspian closed his eyes, waving a hand in dismissal. "I'll visit her soon."

For the first time since Caspian could remember, his father left him alone—simply because Caspian had asked.

Chapter Twenty-Three

TIME PASSED IN A BLUR as a hurricane of thoughts, emotions, and worries raged around Elise, planting her forever in its eye, where she suffered in silent agony. Every day, she dragged herself out of bed and swallowed vitamins, then forced down her throat the healthiest food she could stomach. On days when her meals reappeared—in the most wretched way—she found something else and tried again, no matter how miserable eating made her.

She showered, dressed, tied back the long, red hair that grew noticeably longer and wavier by the day, and wore comfortable shoes that would allow her to remain on her feet. Her tips, she hoarded like a person possessed, each night, shoving the bills by the fistful, into a jar at the back of her closet.

The doctor had found abnormalities in her blood. Maybe it was nothing. Maybe it was something big. Or maybe her child was one quarter to one half Mer—and the only problem with that was that she would never allow anyone take this child from her the way Caspian had been taken from his mother—not even Caspian himself.

She vowed to research, to figure out the species and origin of whatever poisonous creature Caspian's cousin had used to bring her lover ashore in the first place. Somehow, she would find this creature and keep it until her child needed it. She would not be caught unprepared.

Though Caspian had never introduced her to his mother, Elise felt a kinship with the woman, not only because of her love for Caspian, but also knowing that she, too, had carried a child who was part Mer. Only she might know something about what Elise was going through.

Elise stood on the stoop outside the door, hand fisted to knock, but fear held her frozen. The car in the drive was the same one Caspian had left the Turtle in that day, so she knew she was in the right place. But how did one begin the necessary conversation?

Hello, Mrs. Harris. My name is Elise. I'm pregnant with your son's child, do you mind if I come in? Somehow, that approach seemed indelicate for a woman who may, or may not, be scandalized by such a thing. She reminded herself that Mona must have found herself in a similar position at some point—how else had Caspian been conceived?—but without knowing anything about the woman's personality or current beliefs, Elise couldn't bank on any particular reaction.

A flutter in her stomach reminded Elise that her life no longer belonged to her alone, and that quickening bolstered her courage. She rapped on the door, proud to find that her hand remained steady. When no one answered immediately, Elise lowered herself onto the concrete step to wait. Gathering the courage to return would be at least double as hard if she were to leave right now.

Minutes later, the door opened, revealing a willowy lady with thick, dark hair and bright blue eyes. No more than a single wrinkle indented the skin on either side of her eyes, leading Elise to believe that Caspian's mother was much younger than she'd believed.

Mona's lips pinched into what might pass as a smile, had her eyes not radiated grief. "Yes?"

Elise stood, brushing dust from her hands. "Mona Harris?"

Mona blinked, giving no indication of an answer. "Who are you?"

Elise tucked her hair behind her ear, swallowing a lump of apprehension. "My name is Elise. I'm a . . . A friend of your son's. Can you spare a moment to talk?"

Mona's smile grew, if only slightly, and she swung the screen door wider. "I'm pleased to meet you. Won't you come in?"

Elise had worn her favorite yellow sundress, knowing that she would feel more confident sporting something bright and cheery, and as she entered the gloom of the darkened house, found herself grateful for that choice. She sat on the edge of the gray linen couch, while Mona turned an armchair away from the window until it faced the sofa, and then sank into it. She wore flannel pajama pants and a T-shirt, and in the dim light that sneaked through the closed curtains, appeared years older than when standing in the brilliant light of the afternoon sun. "As I'm sure you know, Russell won't be home to visit for several more weeks. What can I do for you, Elise?"

Elise pressed her hands together, and rested them properly on her lap. "Russell?"

Mona blinked, leaning an elbow on the arm of her chair. "My son."

The ends connected in Elise's brain, and she laughed at her foolishness. "Oh, right. Yes. Russell, who's away at college. I'm actually here to talk about Caspian."

"What do you know about Caspian?" Mona's skin paled, her lips pressing into a tight line. "He promised he wouldn't leave without saying goodbye, and I know my son would not lie to me—not about that. Has Tangaroa taken him again? Did you see?"

"I . . . I don't know." Struggling to keep up, Elise stood, desperate for some light, some air, to avoid allowing her stomach to sour. "Is it okay if I open these blinds? I haven't been feeling well, and I'd hate to embarrass myself in your living room." She didn't wait for an answer, and pulled the string, bathing the room in warm daylight.

Mona watched Elise return to her seat, confusion clouding her eyes in the same way grief had, only moments earlier. "I'm sorry, that was rude of me. Let me start again. Tell me, Elise. How do you know my Caspian?"

Although Mona clearly believed that Caspian wouldn't lie to her, it became painfully obvious that he'd told her nothing about Elise.

"We—he's my . . . I guess my boyfriend? If you could classify such a thing. I mean, he's more man than boy, and boyfriend seems like a juvenile term. Especially since we haven't known each other long, but we've become quite close. It's just—I'm sorry, I'm rambling." Her hands trembled, so she tucked them between her knees, only to discover that her knees trembled as well.

Everything about Mona's face, her shoulders, her back, relaxed, degree by degree. "Go on, honey."

236

Elise sucked in another deep breath, frustrated with the way her tongue and brain refused to connect. Never in her life had she struggled to say something of importance the way she did now. "I know where Caspian comes from. Where he's gone."

Mona straightened in her seat, back stiffening as rigid as the chair's frame. "Go on."

Her stomach gurgled with nerves, but Elise pushed forward. "Mrs. Harris, I'm pregnant. Only a few weeks, but Caspian knows, and he's gone to tell his father that he intends to live ashore, permanently, and get whatever poison he needs that will help him breathe here."

Mona blinked, and for a moment, Elise felt as though time stopped, the seconds stretching like taffy on a pulling machine. Finally, the woman responded. "I'm sorry, did you say you're expecting? With Caspian?"

"Yes." Emotion burned behind Elise's eyes, but she held it back as best she could. "I'm so sorry that you had to find out this way, that you and I didn't have an opportunity to get to know each other first or . . . something. But I don't have any family, and Caspian's gone, and even though I know he'll try, I'm not sure if he'll ever be able to come back again, and I—" A sob ripped from her chest. "I'm sorry. The truth is, I'm scared. Terrified."

Mona jumped from her chair and sat next to Elise, wrapping her arms around the girl's shoulders and drawing her in as Elise had always imagined a mother would do. "Shh. Don't cry, darling. I know you're afraid, but you're not alone. Not anymore. I've been in your position. When I first learned I was expecting Caspian, my parents were devastated. There was talk of sending me away, forcing me to give up my child. I couldn't allow that to happen, so I left home. When Caspian was born, we had only each other—and I was too stupid to understand what his father was, or that he might someday return and take my son from me. But I'm older now, and far wiser. And though I don't yet know you well, Elise, I can see that you're far smarter than I was at your age."

Elise sniffled, accepting a tissue Mona offered from the box on the coffee table. "Thank you. I don't feel smart. Actually, I feel dumb that I got pregnant in the first place. It's not like I didn't have tons of birth control options."

Mona rubbed Elise's shoulder, her voice more soothing than anything Elise had imagined from a mother. "My dear, sweet thing, however it happened, this child will come. And if Caspian fails to return to us, we—you and I—will protect this baby. We will not allow the Mer to steal him like they stole Caspian. I swear on my life that if your child ever enters the city of Atlantis, it will be by choice, and not by force."

"I don't know how to prevent it," Elise whispered, admitting her deepest, darkest fear. "What if Caspian tries to take him?"

Mona shook her head. "I don't believe he would, or could do such a thing, but together, you and I will unearth whatever poison can save my grandchild. The Mer will never be able to touch him."

Elise sat at the kitchen table, watching Mona cook with a large degree of guilt. "Are you sure I can't help with something? I'm a halfway decent cook." She'd shown up at this woman's home and interrupted her sleep after a very long hospital shift the night before—only to be immediately cared for as if *she* were an invalid.

Mona replied with a decisive shake of her head. "Nope. You may be part of the family now, but tonight, you're a guest in my home, and you're carrying my grandchild. My first grandchild. You are to sit in that chair and allow your body to grow that baby, while I make you food that I know will stay down. How's your morning sickness?"

Elise scrunched her nose in distaste, hesitant, because she wasn't a huge fan of fish unless it was shellfish, but Mona insisted that seafood was the best meal to satisfy her grandchild—and Elise didn't have the heart to argue. "Not horrible. I don't have much of an appetite. I force food down to give me the energy to get through the work day, and sometimes that force-eating backfires, but most of the time, I do all right."

Mona swirled the frying pan to prevent the halibut skin from sticking to the bottom, then replaced it on the stovetop. "You know, I never liked fish before Caspian, but while I carried him, even though I couldn't stand the smell, seafood was the most reliable, healthy food I could stomach. At the time, I didn't understand that my baby was half Mer—and I'm not sure how I stumbled onto the fish-eating trick, but I've been a lover of all varieties of seafood ever since. Carrying him must have changed my body composition—you know how some women crave pickles or peanut butter? I craved anything from the sea."

The pungent scent intensified, turning Elise's already noxious insides. She covered her mouth, praying that she could make it out of the house before the contents of her stomach made an encore appearance.

"I don't crave anything, yet." *Except Caspian.* His arms, his skin on hers, his breath in her ear, teasing her hair, and sighing against her lips. The craving for him had grown so strong that she ached from the inside out, and he'd only been gone a week.

In another pot, Mona had dumped a concoction of herbs, liquids, seaweed, and what appeared to be a tiny octopus, and now she added lemon juice, stirring vigorously. As if she'd read Elise's mind, Mona said, "If my son says he'll be back, he will. He's a man of his word, my Caspian."

"I believe that," Elise agreed, a note of caution in her voice. "But how long will it take? A year? Five? Ten? It took him twenty-one years this last time—our child will be an adult by then. And I'm not sure I can handle being alone for that long."

Mona's pot slammed against the frying pan so hard that the stirring spoon bounced out and landed on the floor. Shaking her head, Mona opened a drawer and picked out a new spoon, while Elise picked up the escaped one, intending to drop it in the sink. As she stood, a flash of white caught her attention, sticking out from beneath the refrigerator. She grabbed the corner and tugged until it tore free, mostly intact, save a jagged chunk of the corner.

At first, she thought it just a scratch paper on which someone had spun a pen to bring out the ink, but closer inspection revealed something more structured. She squinted, eyes pinned to the page, until she made out letters, and then words. Breath caught in her throat, and left her gasping.

Mona spun to support Elise and lead her back to the chair. "This is why I've told you to stay seated, honey. There's really no predicting when dizziness will hit."

"No, that's not . . ." Elise held out the page. "This was stuck under the fridge. You need to read it."

Mona snatched the paper, peering as if she, too, struggled to make out the rudimentary letters. Elise knew the moment when it clicked into place, because Mona pushed a hand over her hair, also gasping for breath. "This is from Caspian."

Elise nodded. "Yes."

"Sounds like he waited for me as long as he dared— so he wasn't kidnapped, but obviously felt rushed to go back."

Elise smoothed the note on the table, hoping to somehow feel Caspian through the words he'd put so much effort into writing. "What if they keep him there? Imprison him so he can't escape? Then what do we do?" She leaned toward the paper and sniffed, wishing for a trace of Caspian's unique, salty musk. "Is there anything?"

Pale as the dinner plates she removed from the cabinet, Mona flipped off the stovetop and scooped up two healthy portions of fish, topping it with the mysterious side-concoction, which had turned out remarkably creamy and comfortingly herbal-scented. "First we eat. My grandbaby needs nourishment to stay strong. And then we'll visit Caspian's cove. I don't know much about how we can help, but I've got an idea, one I think—I hope—will at least gain the attention of a certain Sea King. I'll find you a jacket to protect you from the cool wind, and we'll bring blankets as well. This could turn into a long night, waiting outside in the chill."

Elise swallowed, trepidation tingling in her neck and shoulders. She was due at the Turtle in an hour. "May I use your phone? I think I'll call in sick to work, and see if one of the other girls is willing to cover for me. My boss knows I'm pregnant, so that won't be a hard sell, as long as I don't leave him in a bind."

Mona set the plates on the table, one in front of Elise, and the other at a vacant spot next to her. "Good idea. I'll make sure we have a comfortable enough setup for you to get some rest. I think having us both present will help persuade the Sea King."

Alarm shot through Elise, and she stood—fast enough to cause spots to bloom in her vision. She grabbed the edge of the table for extra support. "The . . . the actual Sea King? Caspian's father?"

Mona offered Elise an arm and urged her to sit again. "Don't worry, he won't bite. At least, not us." When Elise could only stare in return, Mona added, "Hurry up and eat, before your supper gets cold." She glanced at her watch with a curt nod. "We'll leave in an hour—less if we can be ready to go faster than that."

Elise ate the fish, hardly able to taste it or savor any flavor, but grateful for the warm, home cooked meal that someone else had prepared. Once they'd finished, they each retreated to a room. Elise in Caspian's, and Mona in her own, where they layered on whatever sweaters, hoodies, and thick hats they could find.

Mona packed a beach bag with towels, blankets, and a stack of Caspian's clothes, winding her car keys in hand. "You ready?"

Elise glanced down at her favorite yellow dress, covered over with one of Caspian's new, soft sweatshirts. "I suppose as ready as I'll ever be."

Mona grinned in a way she hadn't since Elise arrived. "I think the two of us will get along very well. Let's go, shall we?"

Chapter Twenty-Four

HE SLEPT ONLY LONG ENOUGH to replenish his energy, dreaming that he held Elise in his arms—snuggled together with their limbs tangled, like pieces broken from the same stone—and woke a short time later to find himself alone. It would not do for him to waste time resting, when he had promises to keep. He rose, and dug into a chest of childhood treasures, looking for some slivers of gold and silver he'd salvaged, long ago, from the wreckage of a sunken ship. Maui had insisted that such things could be used to purchase valuable items, such as off-market or illegal Paihana, jewels the Sea King had not confiscated, rare human commodities brought in by salvagers, and food that originated in far-away seas.

If his coins could purchase such rare, illicit articles as those forbidden in the market, Caspian suspected that they could also purchase information. He hoped he had gathered enough to purchase knowledge of where he might locate Tuck.

Throughout the waking tide, the palace sang with activity and life, making it difficult for Caspian to skulk the passages unnoticed. With his hair shorn in the fashion of humans, he'd set himself apart from the other mermen, leaving him open to more scrutiny than he might already be receiving for his visit ashore. He kept to the shadows—which were few—and the lesser-used corridors, keeping his head down, but always, always aware.

As he crossed a juncture leading into the servants' hall, a unit of guards approached, forcing Caspian to take cover behind a statue of Neptune, his ancestor from long ago. Once the guards passed, Caspian persisted with his clandestine mission, seething inside that he felt such a need for secrecy.

He entered the galley, where food was kept and meals prepared, knowing that the area would be a burrow of activity, with mealtime approaching. A buxom mermaid with bright purple hair and long, talon-tipped fingers ripped apart a wriggling fish and pulled out it's innards, which she tossed to a collection bowl. Across the way, a shorter, stick-thin mermaid with stubby fingers used a sharpened whalebone to chop tentacles off an octopus. Perched on a nearby stool, a young, dark-skinned merman sorted through heaps of harvested clams, prying them open with a pointed narwhal tusk.

All activity ceased the moment Caspian entered, and the mermaid nearest the door scrubbed her hands in a bucket of sand as he approached. "Hello, my Prince. What is your desire this tide?"

Uncomfortable with the confused scrutiny of the galley staff, Caspian reminded himself that he would never know which of these servants—if any—he could trust to remain quiet about his inquiries. Rumor of his search would surely reach the Sea King with the speed of a slithering eel, which gave him yet another reason to hasten his efforts. "I am looking for a friend. A merman called Tuck. I am told he has visited the palace, but resides in the city."

The mermaid blinked, her deep-amber eyes cloudy with confusion. "My Prince, I am sorry. I do not know a merman by that name." Caspian withdrew a small, silver coin from his pouch. "It is important that I find him. Any who shares information leading me to this merman will be richly rewarded." He pressed the coin into her palm. "But my quest must remain a secret from the Sea King, and from my betrothed. Should either of them question my intent, I will offer only punishment to the Mer with the flapping gums. Tell the others."

The mermaid's eyes widened in fear, but she bowed, swishing her tail. "Yes, my Prince. I will bring you word."

Caspian returned to his room to prepare for the meal with his father—and likely everyone else in the palace, assistants, guards, and servants included. He snapped gold cuffs on his wrists, and a royal insignia around one upper arm. He placed his circlet—a thick, gold band, encrusted with pearls and tiny, intricate shells—atop his head, saddened that it did not fit the same as it had when his hair was long and glorious.

He removed it from his head, and was attempting to adjust the pliable gold, when movement drew his attention to the doorway. Had meal time come so quickly? It seemed as though days and nights in Atlantis lasted only half as long as those on land. "I shall join the meal party soon." He kept his focus on the privacy curtain, suspicion boiling inside him.

"I prefer that you remain here a while longer." Marietta pushed through the curtain and into his room, allowing the covering to fall closed behind her. "Welcome home, my Prince. When my father informed me that you had returned, I did not believe it. Since you have not deemed me worthy of a visit, I was forced to come here and see for myself."

"Marietta." Caspian's throat squeezed tight. Having a mermaid in his room would be considered improper, and conveyed the wrong message to any Mer who witnessed that such a meeting had occurred. If anyone suspected that Marietta's honor had been compromised, the time extension Tangaroa had granted against Caspian's betrothal would be withdrawn, and their joining required to take place. He could not allow that.

"I was forced to rest after a long, exhausting journey. I had intended to send word to your father, requesting your company at the end of tide meal." The lie fell off his tongue easily, which was not typical of the Mer. Lying had no place—except obviously here in the palace, where he'd recently discovered truths that rocked his world. He wondered if lying was a human trait, inescapable by even the half-human royals. Or, perhaps the Mer were simply better at hiding their lies. He'd been so innocent before he'd left, and now that he'd returned home, nothing was as it had been. He questioned everything, and everyone.

Marietta pouted, a stream of bubbles rising from her gills. "I am told a servant witnessed you lurking near the galley hall. Has your visit ashore allowed time that you would forget the location of my dwelling?"

He'd known investigating during the waking tide was a mistake. But if he had not gone before the palace occupants slept, he would not have found the galley populated, and he would not know that Tuck does not serve within the palace. Another lie fabricated in his mouth. "I have not been well since my journey. The royal healer allowed me a dose of medicinal Paihana."

The pouting changed to confusion, and then anxiety. "You are not well? Have you brought human disease back with you?"

With this lie, Caspian walked a fine line. Marietta's father led the royal guards and oversaw the Atlantian army, holding substantial influence with the Sea King. Her father's position was the reason Caspian and Marietta had become betrothed in the first place. Any story he fed to her would be relayed—from her, to her father, and then to his father.

Though he yearned to give Marietta any reason for which she might reconsider their imminent joining, he could not risk having his father assign a healer to attend to Caspian's every need.

"No. It is not human disease. Time is kept differently on land, and the exertion of travel has caused me to feel unwell as I re-adjust."

Suspicion burned in Marietta's eyes. She folded her arms across layers and layers of neck adornments. "What variety of Paihana is used for such an ailment, as one caused by a visit to humans?"

He could not tell her, because he did not know. Marietta had already proven herself cunning enough to sneak to the surface and find him as he walked on the beach, so he feared any further lies would only fuel her distrust. Instead, Caspian produced the clamshell filled with the bitter Paihana he'd stolen from Maui's room. "I do not recall the name of this vile concoction, but one drop caused my tongue and lips to numb as it lulled me to sleep."

She bent to closer inspect the red gel, then brushed her hand over his, closing the shell. "You must not spill it, then."

Caspian re-stowed the container in his pouch and offered Marietta his arm, anxious to shoo her from his private space. "Let us attend the meal."

But the sly mermaid avoided his directing grasp, gliding close enough to run her webbed hands over his muscular chest. "The meal can wait. I have not seen my betrothed for many tides. I worried that you might never return."

Never in his life had Caspian been so near to a mermaid, especially not one who used her mesmerizing siren song to tempt him. No man, human or Mer, could easily resist the voice of a siren, but Caspian gave it a desperate effort as Marietta twisted her tail around his legs and slid her body along his skin in invitation.

She skimmed her lips along his collar bone and neck, drawing his ear into her mouth with a deliberate purr of pleasure as her lips overtook his, and her tongue invaded his mouth. Though his thoughts spun with confusion, he willed his body to remain unresponsive—but his body refused to comply. She tangled herself around him, wrapped them in her hair as she attempted to fully consume him with lust. Caspian might had fallen prey, if not for the salty tang of her tongue, which snapped him back into himself. This sensation was not familiar or sweet, as he'd come to expect from a kiss. Everything about the experience struck him wrong.

A gurgling sound rose in Marietta's throat, similar to the cry of a human baby, and Caspian wrenched himself away as his memory filled with Elise. "Stop." He bellowed, backing to the door and brushing the curtain aside. "You must leave me, now. This moment. I will not be lured to temptation. Do not return to my cavern again."

The pout from earlier returned as Marietta slinked into the hallway. "We are to be joined soon. I do not understand the need to wait."

Caspian urged her forward, remaining behind her so she could not catch him off guard again. "I will not dishonor my father, or my status as Prince of this city. You must not attempt such a thing again."

She didn't reply, leading Caspian to believe that she wouldn't give up easily. He would have to work harder to avoid Marietta.

The market in Atlantis had not changed much during Caspian's time away, nor had the goods sold there, but as he traveled the familiar paths, he felt as though he was seeing the city for the first time. He used to enjoy visiting the markets, especially the booths run by scavengers, who scoured the far, wide sea to transport items left behind by sunken human ships. Each broken fragment of pottery had reminded Caspian of his life before Atlantis, and he'd treasured those memories, those items, as mementoes of a place to which he might never return. But now he had new memories, fresh and painful ones that fueled his desperation to return to his new home ashore.

Rather than cheerful merchants and colorful wares, he saw drab, angry faces of traders, desperate to win the King's favor. They adopted a happy façade the moment they caught sight of Caspian's circlet and realized who he was, then they endeavored to peddle their most expensive pieces of junk to him.

Instead of shiny, beautiful edifices, covered with lovely plants and natural shells, he now saw run-down buildings, on the verge of collapse from the weight of barnacles that had grown over the walls and rooftops.

Now that he'd spent time ashore in Oceanside, he recognized differences in class, culture, and habit—behaviors from which he'd been sheltered during his childhood of privilege. The Atlantis his father had raised him to believe in was little more than a fairytale, a Utopia of dreams, and far-removed from reality.

An aged merman, wrinkled and sagging, seized Caspian's arm, cupping a broken shell between his webbed fingers. "Spare a coin to buy Paihana for an elder?"

Caspian rested a hand on the merman's shoulder, digging into his pouch for a coin. "Sir, do you know of a merman called Tuck?"

The man shrugged him off, ignoring the question. "Coin for Paihana? Please, sir. The Sea King has taken my home and left me with nothing."

There were a lot of things Caspian currently questioned about his father, but this issue he did not. The Sea King had never taken anyone's home—it was a point of pride for which he'd boasted for as long as Caspian could remember. Tangaroa had no use for the shelters belonging to citizens of Atlantis, and one of the things he'd drilled into Caspian's head was the importance of all citizens being provided with safe dwellings. He dropped the coin back in his pouch, feeling used. "My father does not take homes. You, sir, speak in fiction. I will not donate coin to a fraud."

Startled, the man drew back, his gaze traveling Caspian's length. "You are not the Prince. Our Caspian wears the long, dark hair of a royal."

Not wanting to draw attention to himself, Caspian withdrew, progressing down the path, where he witnessed more interactions like the one he'd just experienced. The city he'd once believed so perfect had an underside that palace-dwellers never saw. Perhaps their community was not as abundant as his father believed.

Over six waking-tides, he searched for Tuck. Each tide, he swam a different route, traversed different paths and areas where he'd never explored, aimlessly wandering, inquiring of the Mer who did not recognize him as Prince. On the sixth tide, he encountered a tavern, overflowing with patrons, who laughed and danced, singing along to the music of the Mer band playing inside. Hundreds of Mer had squeezed into the small space, their revelry spilling into the waterway, where the celebrating continued. The crowd did not thin, even as sleep-tide approached, indicating that none intended to prepare for bed.

Caspian squeezed inside, astounded to find the tavern much bigger than it had first appeared. He scuttled around drunken Mer and skillfully maneuvered into a spot at the bar, which came available when the merman who had occupied the stool passed out and drifted toward the ceiling.

The tavern was set up similar to the clandestine Paihana parties Caspian had attended in the galley wing of the palace, during the time when Maui lived there. Behind the bar stood a tall ice edifice, carved with lines upon lines of shelves, which displayed a variety of Paihana in various colors, containers, and strengths. The muscular merman behind the counter wore no coverings, except the identifying cuffs of a tender. He swam for the top-most shelf, from which he plucked a slim cylinder of deep-green gel. He then returned to the long, stone platform, where he scooped portions into the clay vessels used for serving.

Once he'd allocated the portions, he floated to Caspian, drawing his lips into a smile similar to those worn by the market merchants. Caspian hid his disappointment by focusing on the bottles and jars, hoping to find his favorite—a red-color Paihana with a hint of sweetness and a dash of heat.

"Would you like the tide special?" The tender set an empty vessel in front of Caspian.

Caspian inspected the vessel, surprised to discover that rather than clay, it was made of iron—heavy enough to stand upright, regardless of disturbances in the water. "Which one is the special?"

The tender sliced a thick vein of gel from a block of yellow and plopped it into Caspian's cup. "Taste of the sun. I'm told this is a favorite in Oceania."

Caspian's ears perked with attention. Maui had come from Oceania, and immigrants from there rarely visited Atlantis, nor did they stay long when they did. "Oceania? Have you been there?"

"I have." The tender shook his head, urging Caspian to sample the special. "That is where a close friend and I first discovered the benefits of Paihana. My tavern offers formulas not seen or tasted anywhere else, which is clearly why my tavern is so well attended."

Caspian lifted the vessel and let the yellow gel slide down his throat, finding it quite pleasant. "Yes, I shall take a portion of this."

Without waiting for more discussion, the tender sliced a larger portion from the block and laid it into Caspian's cup. "Anything else?"

"You seem to know much of what happens in this section of the city." Caspian slid a weighty gold coin onto the stone counter, keeping two fingers on top of it until the tender's eyes widened with interest. "I am looking for a merman called Tuck, and I must find him soon."

The tender's eyes darted around, as if he worried about who was watching. He lowered his voice. "Finish your drink and leave this place. Go now, and return after the toll of the sleeping tide." His eyes flicked to the gold. "That might not be enough to convince this Tuck to reveal himself, and if he does, it will not compensate him for the thing you seek."

Surprised Caspian, covered the coin with his palm. Coins of all varieties were rare and valuable, and the gold ones more than most. "What makes you believe I am looking for a particular something?"

The tender leaned closer, shoving aside a sleeping merman who tipped against his shoulder. "Coins may be lovely and rare, but are oft traded within Mer cities. Special favors of the variety provided by Tuck require a more distinctive value."

"Then how shall I prepare to pay him?" Caspian asked, prepared to offer his father's entire jewel collection if necessary.

"All I can tell you is the price will be high." A patron tossed an iron Atlantian coin at the tender, who scooped it out of the water and dropped it into an opaque jar beneath the counter.

"I am prepared to pay whatever is necessary." Caspian swallowed the rest of his Paihana and returned the gold coin to his pouch, instead paying the bill with Atlantian chips, and leaving an extra to purchase the tender's silence. "I shall return after the toll. Thank you, my new friend."

After exiting the tavern, he found a shadowed corner between two structures, where he hid himself among the seagrass, and settled in to wait.

Chapter Twenty-Five

"CAREFUL, MY DEAR, IT'S STEEP." Mona brandished a flashlight, illuminating the path ahead as she led Elise down the precipitous trail to Caspian's cove. "Take extra caution with my grandbaby."

Elise picked her steps cautiously, grateful for the half-moon that provided additional puddles of light. She braced a hand on the sheer cliff, trying not to think about the deadly drop off on her other side. Though the trail narrowed here and there, the majority stretched wide enough to hike without too much risk of sending the women plummeting to the jagged rocks below.

The route didn't get easier at the bottom, pitted with sharp, volcanic rock, and littered with tide pools and vegetation, none of it a flat surface on which to travel. Elise shadowed Mona, surprised as the older woman sprang around each obstacle with the nimble feet and graceful balance of a dancer. When they reached the edge of the sea, Mona wedged her hand into a crevice in the cliff, and swung around the cliff wall, disappearing from view.

Elise imitated her new friend, shoving her hand into the fissure, and then hesitated.

"Here we go." Mona peeked her head around and offered an additional helping hand. "The first time Caspian brought me here, I almost refused to make this leap. But don't worry, there's sand on this side. Makes for a soft landing."

Drawing in a breath of courage, Elise swung around, pleased when she landed with both feet on damp, beachy ground. They'd entered a shallow cave, inside of which had formed a very small, private stretch of beach that could not be seen from the shore. Water lapped at the sand, but even in the dark, the nearby drop-off into deeper water remained visible by the way the water faded from turquoise to indigo. "What is this place?"

Mona brushed off her hands and kicked her shoes aside, digging her toes into the powdery sand. "I call it Caspian's cove. This is where he first emerged when he arrived from Atlantis. I've visited several times since he left, and a few times together with him, and never once have I seen a trace of other people."

Given the area's popularity for tourism, a private space this nice was hard for Elise to fathom. "But there are houses at the top of the trail. And we're not far from the harbor. Surely it can be seen and accessed by boat?" Elise stood at the edge of the sand, peering at the dark swells as they rippled along the moonlit surface.

"I don't know about the people who live in the houses, but I'm certain that they can't see this treasure of a place from where they live." Mona joined Elise at the threshold, directing her attention to dark masses on either side of them. "See there? You're looking at two extended coral reefs, hovering just feet below the water level. They form a barrier that's dangerous for boaters. According to Caspian, this inlet is shallow. Deep enough for swimming, but a boat—even a small one—would run aground." She bent to pick up a handful of sand and let the grains sift through her fingers. "I Googled it once. This cave is documented, but apparently requires too much effort for tourists— or even residents—to visit."

Further toward the horizon, a stone formation rose from the water, probably a mile away, maybe more. It appeared to be a natural stone arch, but with the darkness and the distance, Elise couldn't be sure.

A briny gust of wind picked up her hair and settled it on her shoulders, twisting the ends together. Though she and Mona had packed blankets in anticipation of the chilly fall breeze, adrenaline pinked her skin and kept her from shivering in the crisp, damp air. "It's so peaceful here, and beautiful. Separate from the rest of the world."

Mona trailed her fingers along the wall, walking the length of the cave, and stopping at a natural ledge near the back. "I imagine that's why Caspian emerged here. He must have needed privacy while he oriented himself." She ran her hands over the stone, moving loose rocks from a mound.

Elise joined Mona at the ledge. "What are we looking for?"

Mona rolled aside a large stone, revealing a cutout. "Caspian's things." She stuck her hand in and withdrew a T-shirt, and then a pair of board shorts. "I had to be sure. This is definitely where he went back in, and since he'll need clothes, it's also where he'll come back." She stuck her hand in again, and withdrew Caspian's pendant.

Elise gasped, torn between apprehension and longing. "He never takes that off. Ever. Not even to shower or . . . be intimate." Didn't he need it to breathe? What if it got stolen?

Mona pinched the pendant between two fingers and spread it across the ledge for a closer look. "He claims these pearls have been soaked in some kind of poison that allows him to use his lungs. He must have left it, so that no Mer could steal it. And probably so his gills would function as he passes below."

Elise buried her face in the T-shirt, absorbing the lingering scent of salt and skin and musk that was so uniquely Caspian. Emotions crashed against each other, tangling into a jam in her throat.

Mona's supporting hand swept across her back. "He'll be back, honey. He promised, and I cannot imagine my son not doing everything in his power to get here in time to see his child born."

She spread a blanket on the sand and the two of them settled there, Elise clutching the T-shirt against her chest. "I know he'll try. I know it. But what if it's impossible? What if there's no more poison, or his father holds him captive or, or . . ." she stopped to catch her breath. Suddenly everything about life felt out of her control, and she didn't like that sensation at all.

"He'll get here." Mona stared into the distance, focusing on the stone formation. "Time's an interesting thing. When Tang first took Caspian from me, every day felt like a year. Slow like molasses—no, like peanut butter squeezing through a pinhole. I couldn't eat, couldn't sleep, didn't function, really, except to return over and over again to that beach. I prayed. I screamed. I begged the gods to *give me back my son*." She swallowed hard, and her gaze plunged to the sand, where her fingers swirled intricate circular designs, as if they'd done it from muscle memory.

"After a while, I learned to accept that he was gone, and while I continued to hope, to pray, to wish, I went back to work. I cleaned my house. And after losing more weight than a person my size ever should, I began to eat again. Once a year had passed, time didn't feel quite as slow. I still returned to that beach as often as I could, but I began to date, to attend social gatherings. I forced myself to keep living, and time pushed on. It wasn't long before I married my husband, and then we had Russell." She set a reassuring hand on Elise's forearm. "I *never* gave up on Caspian. Not for one day. I'm his mother, and I knew he'd come back to me when the time was right. And he did."

But it took him twenty years. Elise blinked back tears, though her eyes swelled with pressure. "Thank you for sharing your faith. I don't want you to think that I don't believe in him. I do. I know Caspian will do whatever he can to get back to me. To us." She pressed a hand to her stomach, to the flutters she'd began to feel moving inside it. "But it's different for me than it was for you. I'm left in limbo. If he doesn't come back for a year, do I move ahead with my life? Do I leave Oceanside and go to school? Do I find a man and get married, or should I spend the next ten or fifteen years waiting, and raise my child alone? What if something happens to me? Who will care for our child then?"

"I will. You'll always have me." Mona folded her knees into her chest and rested her chin on them. "Elise, you don't have to know all the answers right now. They'll come to you with time. When Caspian first left, he was six. Too young and too small to escape the Sea King all by himself. He had to grow into his strength, his power, his bravery and wit. That's not the case now. He's grown already, and he came home on his own. I don't believe he'll stay gone anywhere near as long this time, especially knowing that we're waiting for him."

The unspoken fear Elise had held trapped spilled out, leaving her shivering uncontrollably, but not from the cold. "What if he doesn't want to give up his throne for a hapless waitress he barely knows? What if he decides Atlantis is his destiny?"

Mona draped a blanket around Elise's shoulders, tucking it into her arms. "*You're* his destiny, Elise. You and your child. Caspian knows this as much as I do. He was never meant for Atlantis—that's the thing Tangaroa didn't understand. Perhaps this time he'll finally get it."

The moon arced above them, and the atmosphere darkened, inviting millions of stars to flood the violet sky. Eventually, exhaustion won out, and Mona and Elise left the cove to return to their homes. In the following days, both returned to the cove, sometimes together, and sometimes alone—both determined to hold space in the sacred place, as if they'd developed a new religion based on the belief that Caspian would come home. That Caspian, Prince of Atlantis, heir to the Sea King's throne, son to Mona, and father to Elise's child, was not lost to them forever.

"Here you go." Elise delivered two entrees to table six, a man and woman dressed far too formal for the beach. "Is there anything else I can get you?"

"I'd love some ketchup, please." The man shoved a French fry in his mouth.

The woman tapped the side of her glass. "And a refill of my drink."

"Of course." Elise jostled through the swinging door to the kitchen, pausing when pain stabbed her side. She refilled the drink, and snatched a ketchup bottle, delivering both to the table with shaky hands. "There you go. Enjoy." As she straightened, another pain lanced through her. Gasping, she doubled over, gripping the nearest empty table for support.

"Ma'am, are you all right?" The man she'd just served stood, though she couldn't focus on his face.

Struggling to breathe, Elise shook her head no, collapsing to the ground as pain radiated from her core. The woman customer eased her up and into a

266

chair, while the man strode to the back, his phone to his ear.

Marcus, Shelley, and Gina—the newest waitress—rallied, along with the customers. "We should get her to a hospital." Shelley pressed a cold rag to Elise's forehead. "She might be miscarrying."

Hearing that horrid word, Elise blubbered. "No. I'm not. Something's wrong, but that's not it." To prove it, she attempted to stand, ignoring the dizziness that pulled her back down, and the nausea that flushed her face and churned her insides to mush.

An ambulance careened to a stop out front. The paramedics strapped her to a gurney, covering her with blankets, and asking a million questions that Elise's brain couldn't process. The next thing she knew, she was in a hospital exam room, and Doctor Meyer walked in, his usually smooth forehead etched with concern. "Good news and bad news," he said, pulling a stool to the side of Elise's bed. "The nurses who've examined you don't seem to think you've miscarried, so I'm going to use this little device," he held up a small microphone-looking tool attached to a square speaker, "to find the baby's heartbeat. If baby's still alive, we'll know."

He flipped on the device and covered Elise's abdomen with cool, clear gel. Seconds later, a rapid, steady rhythm filled the room, and Elise sighed in relief. "That's it, right? The baby?"

"Yep. And sounds strong, too." He set the heartbeat monitor aside and wiped off the gel with a towel. "So, the good news is that you haven't miscarried."

Elise gulped, though her dry mouth tasted like chalk already. "What's the bad news?"

"It's possible you've been overdoing the physical activity. I'm not ready to put you on bedrest this early in a pregnancy, but I strongly recommend that you cut back on the hours of being on your feet."

A different type of pain gouged Elise, this one through her throat. "I can't afford that. I'm single, and have no help paying bills. I want to go to school. I'm going to be a mother, and children cost money."

Doctor Meyer covered Elise's hand with his own. "I understand. Believe me, I do. And of course, how you deal with this is up to you. But if you were my daughter, I would tell you it's time to apply for government assistance, or go stay with family, if you have any. Or close friends. Maybe sell something you own of value. How you handle this could save the life of your child."

Her stomach felt as though it dropped to the floor beneath her bed. Why hadn't she kept the jewels Caspian had once offered her? "Do you promise this will save my baby's life?"

"No. I'm sorry." He turned away to clean off the heart-monitor machine. "I can't promise anything. But in my medical opinion, it's your best shot."

Mona fluffed the pillow on Elise's bed and tucked the covers around her. "I don't want you to worry about a thing. I'm a registered nurse, and I'm going to camp out here with you for as long as you need me."

Embarrassed to be so weak, Elise patted the comforter next to her, inviting Mona to sit. "You don't have to do that. You have a life, too."

Mona stroked Elise's forehead, tucking her hair behind her ears. "We're family now, and family is my life. I want to be here."

"Thank you. I can't thank you enough." Elise squeezed Mona's hand, wondering how she'd suddenly acquired a mother—another unexpected gift from Caspian. "The doctor says as long as I take it easy until my appointment the next week, I might be able to go back to work on a limited schedule. I won't need round-the-clock care for more than a few days."

Mona stood, replying with the sharp nod of a no-nonsense decision-maker. "When we're certain that you and the baby are both out of danger, then we'll discuss your job. Until then, I'm here. And I'll keep being here." A knock sounded on the door, and Mona stood. "That'll be Marcus. He's called to check on you about every ten minutes since you were released. Shall I let him in?"

"Yes, please." She'd invited Marcus to visit. Aside from Mona, he was the only person she trusted to handle a sensitive and vital task.

Marcus peeked around the door into the room, humming with concern. "How ya doin, kid?"

Elise swept an arm across the lump that was her legs beneath the covers. "I'm alive, and so is baby. That's the important thing."

Marcus crept closer as if he now viewed her as an invalid, squinting through the dim light to better see her pale face. "Don't suppose you'll be back to work anytime soon?"

"Not for a while, I'm afraid." Elise stretched a hand to the nightstand drawer, easing it open to withdraw her father's antique pocket watch. "Marcus, I need a favor."

He sat on the edge of the bed, accepting the watch Elise laid in his hand.

"I need you to sell this for me. Get as much as you can—shop around if you have to. Gold's at a premium right now, and that's an antique, handed down for three generations. Should be worth a decent amount."

Marcus cleared his throat, gaping at the watch. "Elise, why would you sell something like this? It's an heirloom. Don't you want to save it for your baby?"

She choked back emotion, attempting to keep her voice neutral, but failing. "I wish I could, but if I can't work, I can't pay my bills. I need the money to get by, and aside from my car—which is way more useful than the watch—this is the only thing I own of value. Please, don't make this harder than it already is. Just do it, okay? For me."

He closed his hand around the watch, emotion glimmering in his eyes. "Okay. For you. I'll be back tomorrow to check on you. Hang in there, honey. Everything's going to be all right." He bent to hug her, then straightened and strode away, closing the door behind him.

Elise relaxed against the pillows and moved her box of tissues from the nightstand to the bed—utilizing the first one to catch her tears as they fell.

Chapter Twenty-Six

WHEN THE LAST PATRON OF the day had been pushed out the tavern door, Caspian arose from his hiding place, and knocked on the locked wooden panel. The tender peeked out, and after assuring that Caspian had come alone, ushered him inside and then secured an iron bar to hold the panel in place.

"The royal guards do not go easy on establishments that disobey the sleep-tide laws," he explained. "Though, it is not unusual when I am awoken by Mer desiring to purchase more Paihana. I have learned not to answer, most tides."

Caspian claimed a seat on the stool he'd occupied earlier. "Thank you for taking this risk on my behalf."

The tender settled behind his platform, the structure acting as a shield between them. "Before we go further, please explain who you are, and how you came to know the name of Tuck, when you have clearly never met him."

Though he was hesitant to reveal too much of his true identity, time had become a chain of iron that threatened to drag Caspian deeper with each moment that passed. He would never find the poison without taking risks. He exhaled a stream of bubbles. "I am Prince Caspian, son of Tangaroa, and cousin to Maui. I am led to believe that Maui provided an experimental formula, trusted in the care of the merman, Tuck."

The tender folded his arms across his chest. "What type of experimental formula?"

Caspian imitated the move, casually tilting back on his stool. "I must divulge details to Tuck, only, as mine is an important, confidential matter."

Bubbles curled around the tender's head. "Caspian, I appreciate the need for secrecy, but sharing the truth is the only way you will receive your desired information. I wish to help, but you must first affirm certain details."

More frustrated than ever, Caspian leaned against the bar. "Very well. Many tides ago, Maui drove me ashore, where I called on my human mother and . . . while there, fell in love with a human female, with whom I have now joined. I am to be the father of a Halfling, and wish to join my love and complete my existence in a dwelling on land."

The tender's steely glare melted into a smile, and—to Caspian's delight—offered his hand to shake, in the same way as he'd witnessed humans do. "Congratulations on your newfound family," he declared. "I am the Tuck you seek, and it is true that I possess the poison in question."

Caspian embarked for the palace via the underground passage that Maui had secretly used to travel between palace and tavern. Caspian had spent his life exploring the fortress, and had never known such tunnels to exist, nor had he found evidence of them—and he had believed that he knew all the secrets there. But when Tuck guided him to the entrance, Caspian praised Maui, and the brilliant inventions he'd left behind. A single, industrious merman had presented Caspian with a future of opportunity, rather than captivity. He owed his cousin a debt.

At the end of the tunnel, he materialized into a low-traffic path, only meters away from Maui's former cavern. He clung tightly to the pouch that contained the sealed clamshell. He'd purchased it from Tuck, for the price of four gold coins, six silver, and the remainder of his Atlantian chips. No matter the dangers he faced in the coming tides, protecting that clamshell became Caspian's supreme priority, since it held the precious venom he'd come to find.

Instinct begged him to depart straightaway, without goodbye or apology to his father or Marietta. But thoughts of the caged creatures compelled him to complete one final task, by freeing the enslaved beasts, as Maui had been freed him. Doing so would require only moments, and then he could depart from the city with the knowledge that he had performed a final service.

He returned to his cavern for one last look at the place where he'd grown up, trying to decide what—if anything—he should take with him. First, he located a larger pouch—one that strapped across his chest and hung below one arm—and folded the smaller pouch into the bottom. He then chose two long strands of miniature shells—one for Elise and one for his mother. Neither woman was of the Mer, but he'd learned that all females—regardless of species—treasured pretty neck adornments. A single pearl, harvested from a clam as part of his morning meal, rolled onto the ground, and thinking of Elise, Caspian packed it as well. Last, he packed his gold wrist-cuffs, and the circlet that identified him as Prince.

He considered the writings, taken from Maui's dwelling, and determined them too heavy for the journey, and of little value to him once they'd been removed from the water. As the sleep-tide crawled to an end, he hid in a decorative patch of seaweed to one side of his father's elaborate cavern.

Hours later, Glan knocked and was called inside, and soon after, both mermen floated to the throne room at a pace too slow for Caspian's impatient nerves. With his father occupied by Royal affairs, Caspian crept into the luxurious chamber and tossed back the rug, heaving open the hatch.

"Caspian. What are you doing?" The Sea King's voice boomed through the water, unmistakably furious.

With no other option, Caspian held his ground. "Father, I've come to free the creatures."

Tangaroa scratched his head, frowning at the open hatch. "I entertain no captive creatures."

Anger seethed, emboldening Caspian's courage. "I've seen them, father. Just tides ago."

The Sea King tapped his trident against the ground, his eyes sparkling with amusement. "Show me the creatures you believe to be captive, my son, that I might educate you."

Ignoring the warning bells in his brain, Caspian funneled into the dark, cold space, not bothering to bring a light, since his father's trident would be enough. They reached to the room at the end, finding it empty. Caspian gasped, sending streams of bubbles into his shorn hair as he orbited the space. Not a scrap of evidence remained. "Where did they go? What's happened to them? They were here, just tides ago."

Tangaroa rounded on his son. "Why would you enter my private grotto without permission, and when I am not present?"

Nerves tightened Caspian's shoulders, squeezing his neck. Why had he not left Atlantis directly from the tavern? "I . . . I came to inform you that I had returned."

"And what led you to this grotto, which is so rarely used?"

Caspian angled for the exit, preparing to flee. "Father, where have the captive creatures gone? I know they were here."

Glan cleared his throat, folding his hands over his stomach. "Those creatures were not captive, my Prince. They were the experiments of Maui, malnourished and deformed, many requiring substantial tending before being released into the wild sea."

This answer surprised Caspian. He did not want to believe his father a monster, yet, circumstances with this level of convenience only compounded his suspicions. How was it possible to heal and release every deformed creature within the tides since Caspian's return? And now the Sea King had cause for suspicion

"They are freed, then?" Though he suspected that the creatures had simply been moved, he could not investigate, since remaining in the palace would now risk his new future. The time had come to escape.

"The creatures were set free before last sleep tide," his father confirmed, eyes flashing with anger. "Now explain your devious actions."

He had no good answer—at least, not one that would prevent his banishment to the dungeon caves, so decided upon the truth. "Father, thank you for giving me life, for allowing me to experience Atlantis, and our family of Mer, but I do not wish to rule this place, any more than I wish to join with Marietta. I have chosen to return to my home ashore."

The Sea King trembled with anger, sparks flying from his hands, his trident, his fin as he signaled Glan to summon the palace guards. "You . . . you will not leave."

With his pouch secured against his side, Caspian kicked off from the sandy bottom, rocketing through the tunnel and into his father's room. He shoved open the wooden door and jetted through the palace, no longer concerned about who was looking. The guards would soon follow, and regardless of the efforts Caspian would make to evade, the guards would identify his intended destination.

The nearest palace exit was used primarily by servants, but often left unguarded. Caspian exited in a stream of bubbles, a blur of rapid movement. The alarm sounded, guards rushing to heed the call, clouding the water with silt. Meanwhile, Caspian achieved astonishing speeds.

He did not slow to pass through the gate, blowing past the sentries and rocketing into the tunnel like a missile from a ship, ejected with a force driven by desperation, hurtling toward the cove.

Guards emerged, careening from every direction, and forcing Caspian into a high-speed game of cat and mouse that included bolts of lightning, sent to cut down anything that might act as a shield for a lone merman on the run. No coral or reef, no patch of kelp or seagrass or mounds of stone covered in bright growth, was safe from those guards who had been gifted the energy of the stinging eel.

Where Caspian swam, the guards pursued, no speed too quick, no shadow too dark—until there was nothing left for him but to stagger toward the shore. Two of the guards came within arms-length of Caspian's feet—and had his fin reformed, they would have caught hold and towed him back to the city.

The water shallowed as he cut through the narrow pass between coral reefs, and he did not slow until he'd reached the sandy shore and heaved himself out of the water.

"Caspian." A relieved gasp had him spinning around before his feet had oriented, but the voice was one he would never mistake anywhere, at any time.

"Elise." He crossed to take her in his arms, surprised when his mother swung into the cave as well. "Mother!" He wrapped her in his arms as well, more relieved than he dared admit, to again be near them both.

"I've been so worried." Elise sobbed into his shoulder. "I thought you might not come back."

She'd wrapped a blanket around herself, and he rubbed her arms through it, ignoring how his chest tightened and his lungs fought to take in air, while his gills gurgled with need for salt water. "I made you a promise."

"You did." She pressed her lips to his neck, just below the place where his gills bubbled, and abruptly pulled away. "Your pendant. We've made sure it stayed where you left it. You should put it on." Elise dropped her blanket and snatched the pendant from the ledge, fastening it around his neck while spots blinked in Caspian's eyes.

Once he could breathe again, he kissed Elise, who shivered with cold, and re-wrapped her in the thick blanket. "You should be inside, keeping warm."

She swallowed. "I'm supposed to be taking it easy in my bed—doctor's orders—but I've never been good at following directions. Especially since you walked into my life."

Caspian tugged on his shorts, determined to get Elise home and into a warm tub—which he hoped to share—when a commotion splashed through the shallow waters.

"Caspian," his mother called. "Come. Your father has arrived. It's time to resolve the direction of your future, once and for all."

Chapter Twenty-Seven

ELISE STUMBLED BACK, BRACING HERSELF against the stone wall, her insides fluttering as though a swarm of butterflies wanted to beat through her skin. She covered the gentle swell that would soon become a baby bump. The Sea King and his soldiers would *not* take her child.

"Hello, Tangaroa." All traces of mild sweetness disappeared from Mona's voice as she straightened, pulling her shoulders back, and folding her arms over her chest as if to defend her heart all over again. "I would say it's nice to see you, but we both know I'd be lying."

"Mona." Upon hearing the familiar voice, the Sea King froze in place, his guards reluctant to advance without lead or command. He stood in the shallows only yards away, shoulders and torso exposed to the cool air, and his long hair dripping with water.

She inched toward the edge. "I've waited so long for this moment, wondering how I'd react. I used to imagine myself making threats, or sometimes pleading for you to bring my son home." Caspian joined his mother on the sand, and Mona reached out to squeeze his hand. "But threats and pleading are no longer necessary. He's come home to me on his own."

Elise stayed in the shadows, hoping to avoid the Sea King's notice. Caspian and Mona's shadows formed a solid wall on the sand below them. If they looked as intimidating from the front as they did from Elise's angle, she couldn't imagine a guard—or a Sea King—brave enough to force them apart.

"Father." True to his role of Prince, Caspian took the lead. "I have chosen to abdicate my throne, and make a life here in Oceanside."

With a torrential splash, the Sea King hauled himself out of the sea and onto his feet—naked, as Caspian had been—his wide, muscular shoulders pulsing with anger, and long hair blowing in the crisp breeze. "Caspian, you are Prince of Atlantis, and the only heir to the throne. I cannot allow this."

"I am not asking your permission." Caspian stood his ground, calm and unquestionable. "My choice has been made. I am staying with my mother, who I have longed to be near for all of my life in the sea, and my beloved, Elise, who will soon bear our child."

The Sea King's eyes flicked toward her, then away. Elise cowered. "You are to become a father?"

"I am, yes." Caspian beckoned for her to join him, and so she did, trembling with apprehension until he pulled her into his side. "Elise and I have joined, mated for life, and our union cannot be undone."

"No. This cannot be. It must not be." Electricity shot from the Sea King's fingertips, and Caspian took a protective step in front of Elise, blocking her from harm.

"Tang, stop it." Mona thrust herself between the two mermen, **who** both flashed with jolts of lightning. "Leave them alone." She shooed Caspian and Elise to the back of the shallow cave. "Give us a moment. I need to have a word with your father."

The sparks died from the Sea King's fingers, and his eyes softened as if he'd stepped back in time to a long-forgotten memory. "Mona."

"Tang." She didn't smile, or show a single sign of affection for the man who had abducted her child so many years ago—the man she'd once loved. "Listen to me. Caspian was never meant to live below. His human side has overpowered the Mer. Can't you see that our son has found happiness here? You kept him from me when he was small, but I won't allow you to do so again. It's my turn to know him now."

Distracted, the Sea King gazed at his long-lost lover. "I have often wondered what has become of you."

"I haven't forgiven you, Tangaroa, and I won't." Mona's bright eyes bore into the Sea King as if their power, alone, could burn him to the ground. "You broke my heart into a million pieces, but I found a new love, had another son, and never, for one day, for one moment, have I stopped hating you for taking Caspian away. I've spent my whole life searching, and now that I have him back, I won't let you deprive me of his love ever again."

Tangaroa's face hardened. "You cannot stop me now, any better than you could before."

"Oh, but I can." She opened her palm, revealing a palm-sized waterproof sports camera—the red light indicating that it was recording. Mona's lips bowed, but it wasn't a happy, affectionate smile, so much as one of vengeance, finally disbursed. "Do you know how many billions of humans live on land these days, Tang? More than can be counted. Humans have made incredible technological advancements. We have the power to do all sorts of incredible things. For instance, we have the power to direct a war missile into an underwater city." She tapped a tiny screen on the camera that left no question of the footage she'd already captured. "Machines that take live film, proving the existence of the Mer. We even have watercrafts that can be manned, and driven far enough below to infiltrate your city. We are a people of war, when necessary, and forcefully imprisoning a human—even a halfling-human—is provocation enough."

"Do not attempt to intimidate me." The guards surged closer, but Tangaroa commanded them to stand down with a wave of his hand. "Humans are not a danger to us. Our species is far superior, as has been proven again and again since the evolution of Mer."

She laughed, the sound of a woman on the verge of madness—or one who knew she'd won a long-anticipated battle. "Clearly, it's been a while since your theory was tested. Have you any idea, the power of a single human these days?" She shook her head, not waiting for an answer as she whipped out her phone and opened an app, angling it at the Sea King, so he could witness the delayed footage of himself, followed by all the guards who had accompanied him. "This moving picture will go viral. With one finger swipe, every land in the world will witness footage of you and your people emerging from the sea. They will see your scales, your talons, your oddly colored skin, and they will know that Mer exist. They will also know *where* you exist. As you've apparently indoctrinated my son, I don't have to tell you that humans fear cultures that they don't understand. You must realize that such evidence could mean the end of the Mer."

She paused, allowing that knowledge to sink in. "Not simply Atlantis, either, but all the cities of Mer throughout the world. We will wage war against those who might come for our children, and we will destroy you. Your people will be no more."

Though the Sea King did not show signs of fear, his eyes remained locked on the screen, watching the picture of himself emerging from the water and standing on legs covered in shiny, gray scales. "You would destroy the land where our son shall rule?" He reached for the phone, as if touching it could destroy the threat inside it.

Mona locked the device and shoved it back in her purse. "I will destroy the land of the merman who stole my son. I *will* destroy you, Tang. I've waited twenty-long years for this moment, and I'm prepared to follow through. However, since my son has returned to me, and to his wife-to-be, I'm willing to show a degree of mercy—on his behalf, and on the behalf of his child. If that's what he wants."

The Sea King turned his attention on Caspian. "My son. You are Prince of Atlantis. What say you of your . . . of this female's threats?"

Terrified of what was to come, Elise pressed closer to Caspian's side, absorbing strength from his muscles, his nearness, and the fact that he'd come back to her by choice—that he now defied his father to stay.

Caspian wrapped his arms around her, shielding her, while fitting together as one. "I do not wish my mother to bring harm to Atlantis, or the Mer, but I will not be forced to take your throne. I wish to live as a human, with my human family. You will no longer keep me from them." He stuck his hand into his pouch and withdrew the brilliant diamond his mother had given him. "I offer this stone in trade for my freedom. It is of great worth to humans. Allow me to remain here, Father, and my mother will protect the Mer, as will I."

The Sea King seized the diamond, eyes shining with glee as he turned it over in his hand. "However beautiful, one small stone cannot replace a Prince."

"You'll not have me anyway, father," Caspian murmured. "If you force me to return to Atlantis, to live without Elise, I will die of heartbreak."

"Tang." Mona turned off the camera and stowed it in her purse with the phone. "Let him go. The same way you let me go. Only, unlike me, you have an opportunity to say goodbye, and to keep in touch if you want that." She dumped the pouch of remaining jewels into her palm, reminding him of what he'd left behind. "I'll leave these jewels here, where your guards will see them. When they do, you will know to find us here. Caspian will always have the option to return to Atlantis if he ever decides. If that time ever comes, you'll have enough warning to welcome him home properly."

Tangaroa wheezed, his time spent out of water wearing on him. "What am I to do without an heir? Who will rule Atlantis when I pass?"

Caspian dropped his arms from Elise and removed the golden cuffs, and the circlet from his pouch. "You will find another heir. Maui is blood. If he returns, he might wish to rule Atlantis. Or perhaps there is another. Send your guards to Oceania to seek the children of Tangaloa, and offer them my Princely cuffs. You will have an heir, be he a son, a nephew, or a female descendant. Of this, I am certain."

The Sea King pinned Elise with an intimidating glare that sent a fissure of fear directly to her core. He may be willing to acquiesce for now, but he was not giving up forever.

"You are right, my son. One way or another, I will have my heir. Even if she comes to Atlantis further down the line." Tangaroa stepped to the edge of the water, slipping his treasures into a pouch at his waist. He glanced over his shoulder at Caspian. "Find your happiness, my son, for you will never prosper here in the way you could in Atlantis."

Caspian held out a hand in what Elise assumed a traditional farewell signal. "Be well, father. Please deliver my regrets to Marietta. Perhaps she, too, might find a suitable mate someday."

Tangaroa spent one last gaze on Mona. "You are a human who was meant for the deepest blue sea, and I am a merman, meant to leave my heart on the sandy shore. Since you, I have never loved another. I was not able to stay, as Caspian is, for I was not provided the ability to breathe. Forgiveness has been far and long in coming, but I hope someday you will find it. For your benefit, and that of our son, and grandchild." The Sea King dove into the shallow inlet, moving faster than Elise had ever seen anything swim, and she'd lived near the ocean her entire life.

Her body quivered as she clung to Caspian. "He intends to take our baby."

Caspian rested his chin on her head, stroking her back. "Do not worry about that now. I have learned many things from my visit to sea. When he appears to persuade our child, we will be prepared."

"Yes." Mona continued to focus on the ripple that was Tangaroa and his guards. "We will. As long as I live, the Sea King will never steal another person I love."

Caspian retrieved his shirt, yanking it over his head, as he slid on his sandals. "Come, my love. Come, Mother. Let us go home. I wish to join with Elise immediately, but I do not know much of human matrimonial customs."

Mona turned, her answering grin larger than any Elise had seen from the frail woman. "Don't you worry about that. Elise and I will pull something together."

Chapter Twenty-Eight

PLANNING A WEDDING IN FEWER than twenty-four hours presented a challenge or two. Or many. Though his mother still had not "introduced" them, Caspian called Russell and personally invited his one and only brother to witness his upcoming nuptials. Unfortunately, Russell was unable to come home again on such short notice.

"I'm so sorry I can't be there for you, Caspian," he said. "Really, really sorry. But I know you feel rushed, and I don't want you to wait on my behalf. Marry that girl, be happy while you can. Life is too short to put off something so important, especially when you're expecting a little one."

"I am sorry, too, my brother." When a hint of sadness threatened, Caspian shoved it aside. This was a happy occasion, even without the presence of his newly discovered brother. "I do not know human customs well. Will you instruct me on what I must do? How I should behave?"

Russell laughed. "Oh dear. I've never been married, so I honestly don't know much more than you do. I'll tell you that it's important to say something about how and why you love Elise, and how long you intend to keep loving her. So maybe prepare that, if you can. And when the preacher asks if you'll take her for your wife, you tell him yes, or I do."

"Okay," Caspian said, committing the advice to memory, as he was still not skilled at writing.

"You should buy her a ring," Russell said. "Doesn't have to be expensive, but something nice. Something lasting. It's a symbol of your unending love, and a representation that she's taken—so other men will know as well."

This sounded like a brilliant plan to Caspian. "Where am I to purchase such a trinket, and how am I to pay?"

Russell inhaled a deep breath. "Rings can be pricey. In fact, women are pricey, and children too, from what I hear, so you'll need to get another job, and soon. Until then, if you have anything valuable—pearls or gold, or one of those gemstones like the one you gave to your father—you can take it to a jeweler and see if they'll buy it from you. Take Mom, so they don't try to soak you."

Caspian laughed. "I don't mind being wet."

"Yeah, that's not what I mean. Just take Mom. Let her help you. She's good with valuables."

Caspian heeded his brother's advice, and while Elise met with Marcus to finalize plans, Caspian and his mother journeyed to a seedy area of town, and a jewelry store with bars on the door and windows. There, Caspian offered up the remaining gems he'd once offered to Elise as a gift.

A hefty man who reeked of body odor, wearing a dirty T-shirt and sporting greasy, blue hair, pinched the gems, one by one, between his fat fingers. "High quality," he said. "Older cuts?"

"Of course," Caspian told him. "These jewels have been in trapped in the below for many years."

Mona stomped Caspian's foot. "What he means is that they're rare, antique stones—you don't see a lot of natural ones like these anymore."

The man spread the jewels across a black, velvet tray and pressed a jeweler's loop against his eye. "I'll need to test them, of course, but ballpark, I'd say the entire lot's worth a duce—maybe more."

Mona narrowed her eyes, the fury of her determination skewering the hapless jeweler. "First of all, "duce" is not a well-known professional term. Second, I know my gemstones, and I've done the research. This collection is worth three times the twenty grand you're claiming. Now, I understand that you're in this business to make a profit, and that we aren't likely to get full market value on such short notice—but, if you can't at least come closer to reality, we'll be forced to take these rare, and highly precious gems elsewhere."

The man covered the jewels with his hand and drew the velvet pad nearer to him. "I don't know, lady. I could lose my job if I give you too much."

Caspian reached across the counter and retrieved his gems, an errant electrical spark lighting them through and showering the shop with a rainbow of color. "We shall go elsewhere. Thank you for your time." He took his mother's elbow and escorted her to the door.

"Wait." The salesman rushed around the counter, frustration evident in his movements, but his eyes locked on the gem-filled pouch in Caspian's hand. "Let me make some calls and see what I can do."

While they waited, Caspian wandered the store, wondering what type of ring his Elise might like. While perusing the cases, he came across a pocket watch that looked very much like the one Elise had kept in her nightstand drawer—the one that had been her father's. When the man came back, before he could speak, Caspian jabbed his finger on the glass. "I would like to see this."

The man brought it out of the case, and Caspian turned it over, recognizing the inscription on the back.

Elise had sold her father's watch while he was away. "I wish to purchase this."

The man's forehead wrinkled in confusion. "Okay. Do you want to know my offer on your jewels, or what?"

"Yes," Mona answered. "First, let's hear that offer."

"My boss has authorized me to give you forty-five, but I'd take a thousand off for that." He jutted his chin at the watch.

Mona held the pouch aloft, swinging it to prove the hefty weight. "Forty-eight, and you throw in the watch as a gesture of good faith."

"And a ring." Caspian pointed at a delicate gold band. "This one here." He withdrew a pearl from his pocket—the single pearl that had made it out of Atlantis with him, and which had not been soaked in poison. "And I wish to have this pearl attached to the gold. Today, if you are able."

Another ten minutes of negotiating, and Caspian left the shop with Mona, who drove him directly to a bank, and helped him set up an account. "I'm proud of you, son," she said, beaming with pride and contentment. "Just arrived in town, and already worried about providing for your family. I think, no matter what line of work you go into, you're going to be just fine."

Caspian grinned, happier than he'd ever been. "Thank you, Mother. I do not believe anyone has been proud of me before." Indeed, this closeness was something he had not realized he missed.

She stood on tiptoe and pressed a kiss to his cheek. "Get used to it. I intend to tell you every day."

"Perhaps you will tell me tomorrow, when we return to that shop and pick up Elise's ring."

Mona slid her arm around her son's slender waist. "Of course. And the ring is going to turn out lovely. Elise is going to love it."

Caspian married his sweetheart on the beach, in front of The Sea Turtle. He'd given his females exactly two days to make their plans, and somehow, they pulled off an elegant, private party, complete with ribbons and flowing curtains, twinkling lights and fresh flowers. Marcus even prepared mini-specialty burgers and cakes, and provided a delicious punch that even Elise could drink.

Mona dressed her son in a suit from Russell's closet, and Elise wore a filmy, white dress that brushed the sand as she walked—a dress that had belonged to her mother.

Shelley attended, and Marcus, along with the rest of the restaurant employees, and Caspian's friends from the resort. The only person not present, who Caspian wished had been able to come, was Russell.

Though they'd spoken on the phone just that morning, he felt a strong desire—a responsibility—to write his brother a letter, addressing his last, remaining concerns. As Russell had pointed out, life was unpredictable.

He wrote:

My dear brother Russell,

On this day I am joined to my beloved Elise. I wish you could be present. I am grateful to know I have a brother, and wish to beg one last service from you. The venom I collected from Atlantis is untested, and in the event that something horrible takes me from my new family, please care for my sweet Elise and our child. I do not wish them left without family.

If my son or daughter is born of Mer blood, someday, he or she will eventually be forced to swim in salt water as a matter of survival. Please help Elise and mother find another supply of poison, that my child will know that he or she always has a choice—and that my father, the Sea King, cannot forcefully take that child below. I hope that mother will assist you in this search, as in caring for my family.

Hoping to see you again soon, for an official meeting with our mother.

Your brother eternally,
Caspian

The end.

About Nichole Giles

NICHOLE GILES, author of the *Descendant* trilogy, and the *Water So Deep* series, has lived in Nevada, Arizona, Utah, and Texas. She is a fan of all things paranormal and magical, and her dreams include raising a garden full of fairies, riding a unicorn, and taming the pet dragon she adopted at a recent local ComiCon. She loves to spend time with her husband and four grown children, travel to tropical and exotic destinations, drive with her convertible top down—even when it rains— and play music at full volume so she can sing along.

Acknowledgements

There are days when I feel like the luckiest woman alive, because I get to do this author thing for reals. Other days, I question my own sanity because authoring is not easy. In fact, it's extremely hard about ninety-five percent of the time. When it's hard, that's when I feel luckiest, because I have so many people who are always willing to jump in and help paddle my boat when it starts to sink.

I absolutely could never in a bajillion years do this thing without the love and support of my family. I don't know what I did to deserve them, but they have earned an ocean of thanks. My husband, Gary, my children Brayden, Brittany, Madison, and Mckay, and most recently, my new sons-in-law, Trey and Richie— you seven are my inspiration, my motivation, and my world. I love you more than every grain of sand on every beach in the world.

My extended family also gets a shout out. In a year when the world *overwhelm* is not a strong enough description of my life, my family swept in and tossed me every life preserver they could find. I'm going to name them all, so brace yourselves. Joe (Dad) and Pam (Step-mom), Deanne (Mom) and Steve (Step-dad), Ryan, Matt and Nichole (Tyce and Coleman), James,

Jodi and Nick (and Colby, Kinsey, Kenedy), Chandi (Lacey, Brooklyn, Carver), Zack, Daeton (Charlie), Justin, Cameron, Troy and Anna (and Alex and Isaac). My in-law family, Craig and Keeley, Jalayne and Mike, Jennifer and Rick, and JoAnna, and the late Kay and Carol Giles. Also, my grandparents, who always, always play a role in my stories. Jeneal and the late Mel Petersen, and Mona and Ernie Ketchum. Yes, they are all mine. And not only do I claim them, but I'm proud to do so.

I have the best friends ever. Special thanks to Michelle Argyle, for awesome support and brilliant cover design and story inspiration that is over-the-top helpful, Elana Johnson for always being there, Jenn Johansson who is always good for at least a full day of giggles, Julia McCracken for shag-rug snow angels, Jaclyn Weist for solid, sweet friendship and support, Heather Justesen who is always, and always will be, my writer's knight in golden armor—she has saved me more times than I can count. Tristi Pinkston for helping shape me into the writer I've become, the late Keith Fisher, who was my personal teddy bear cheerleader, James Dashner who has never once given up on me or my ability, despite me giving up on myself. Brekke Felt for endless, unwavering support that's always like a buoy in an endless sea. Lauri Schoenfeld for stepping in when she didn't even know how badly I needed a friend, Rebecca Rode for pushing me to submit to the Shattered Worlds Boxed set, which required that I write this book in the first place, and Lindzee Armstrong for stepping in when I was close to missing my deadline, and saving my formatting bacon. Also, to my fellow Shattered Worlds authors, thank you so much for letting me be a part of something awesome—we did it!

I could go on, but the deadline is looming. I hope, hope, hope that even if you aren't named here specifically, every one of you who has been a part of my author life knows how much I love and appreciate you! Because I truly, truly do.

Thank you for giving me another chance to entertain you.